KILLER: 6 . . . LAWMEN: 0

"The police in this part of the world—and the country—believe in facts."

"Well, it's a fact that this man has killed six people in London. I've brought newspapers that can attest to that."

"That's good," Clint said, "but it won't prove to them that he's here."

"What do you suggest we do?"

"Let's check some back newspapers first," Clint said. "If he *has* killed already, the police here might welcome some help."

"And if he hasn't?"

"I'm afraid they'll claim there's nothing for them to act on," Clint said.

"Until he actually does kill again?"

"Yes."

"You have some strange customs in America, Clint."

"David," Clint said, "I'm afraid they're only going to get stranger for you."

DON'T MISS THESE
ALL-ACTION WESTERN SERIES
FROM THE BERKLEY PUBLISHING GROUP

THE GUNSMITH by J. R. Roberts
Clint Adams was a legend among lawmen, outlaws, and ladies. They called him . . . the Gunsmith.

LONGARM by Tabor Evans
The popular long-running series about U.S. Deputy Marshal Long—his life, his loves, his fight for justice.

SLOCUM by Jake Logan
Today's longest-running action Western. John Slocum rides a deadly trail of hot blood and cold steel.

BUSHWHACKERS by B. J. Lanagan
An action-packed series by the creators of Longarm! The rousing adventures of the most brutal gang of cutthroats ever assembled—Quantrill's Raiders.

THE GUNSMITH

213

STRANGLER'S VENDETTA

J. R. ROBERTS

J

JOVE BOOKS, NEW YORK

STRANGLER'S VENDETTA

A Jove Book / published by arrangement with
the author

PRINTING HISTORY
Jove edition / October 1999

The Penguin Putnam Inc. World Wide Web site address is
http://www.penguinputnam.com

ISBN: 0-515-12615-2

A JOVE BOOK®
Jove Books are published by The Berkley Publishing Group,
a division of Penguin Putnam Inc.,
375 Hudson Street, New York, New York 10014.
JOVE and the "J" design
are trademarks belonging to Penguin Putnam Inc.

PRINTED IN THE UNITED STATES OF AMERICA

10 9 8 7 6 5 4 3 2 1

PROLOGUE

Chief Inspector James Reed looked across his desk in his office at Scotland Yard, quizzically regarding his protégé, Detective Inspector David Frost.

"What is it, David?" the older man asked. "What's troubling you?"

"I know he's out there," Frost said, his hands clasped behind his back, "and he's laughing at me."

"David, you're taking this entirely too personally," Reed said. "The man's a killer, pure and simple. Perhaps even a brilliant one. But don't start to believe that he's killing people just to get at you. That would be . . . well, paranoid."

Frost turned and glared at his mentor. Though barely thirty, he was already a detective inspector at Scotland Yard. Tall, handsome, normally practical, his future was bright—of that there was no doubt. But one mistake now could ruin it all.

However, Chief Inspector Reed's definition of a mistake and Detective Inspector Frost's definition were two entirely different things:

Reed thought it would be a mistake for Frost to get too personally involved in the search for this killer.

Frost thought it would be a mistake to let this killer get away.

"I know where he's gone," Frost said. "That's the problem."

"Where, then?"

"America."

"What?" Reed exclaimed.

"My source tells me he got on a ship to America," Frost said.

"Well," Reed said, "if that's accurate then good riddance. Let the Americans have him."

"No," Frost replied. "I can't let them have him, because he's mine."

"David, how would you ever find him there? It's a big country."

"He's going to New York."

"How do you know?"

"I just do, sir," Frost said. "He's gone to New York City and I must go and get him."

"David, you know I cannot authorize that."

"Then I'll have to go without your authorization, sir."

"Inspector," Reed said, "I must warn you that if you do this, you will be jeopardizing your entire career."

"I know it, sir."

"Is one man worth that?"

"This is not a man, sir," Frost replied. "This is a killer, an animal, and he must be stopped. *I* must stop him."

"David . . ." Reed began, shaking his head.

"I'll be leaving in the morning, sir."

Reed studied the young man for a few moments, then said, "I wish you luck, David."

"Thank you, sir."

"Of course, you realize you'll have no official standing in America."

"Yes, sir," Frost said, "I realize that."

"And I'll have to ask you to leave your credentials here."

Frost hesitated, then removed his wallet and left his credentials on his superior's desk. With that he turned on his heel and walked out, leaving Chief Inspector James Reed to wonder if he'd ever see the younger man again. A finer prospect as a policeman he had never before come across. Now the young man might be throwing it all away, and there was nothing he could do about it.

Or was there?

Reed opened his top desk drawer, withdrew a piece of writing paper, grabbed his quill from his inkwell, and began to write.

"Dear Clint . . ."

ONE

Clint Adams looked once again at the message in his hand. It was from Chief Inspector James Reed, a man he'd met and worked with when he'd gone to London, England, for a gun expo several years back. Reed wanted Clint to meet and take under his wing a young man named David Frost, who was one of Reed's best young detectives. According to the message—which Reed had wired across the ocean before Frost's arrival—the young detective was coming to America without credentials, simply as a private citizen who, as Reed put it, was on a "vendetta." A brief description of Frost followed, and that was it.

The message had gotten to Clint while he was in Chicago, forwarded from Labyrinth, Texas, by his friend Rick Hartman. Clint didn't think he'd arrive in time, but he did—*just* in time. Reed had given him Frost's date of arrival, which had been yesterday, but something had held the ship up until today, enabling Clint to get there.

The Manhattan dock was crowded with people meeting friends and loved ones who were either coming to visit or were returning home from a visit. There were a lot of them, they were getting in Clint's way, *and* they knew who they were looking for.

Clint finally decided to take up a position by the cabstands. The man was going to have to get transportation from the docks to a hotel.

Reed's description of Frost had been simple: blond, tall, slender, handsome. Away from the crowds on the dock Clint was able to spot the man as soon as he approached the cabs. He was carrying one leather suitcase, and was wearing a top hat and a cape.

Clint moved to intercept Frost before he could get into a cab.

"Mr. Frost?"

The man stopped short and studied Clint with a policeman's eyes, trying to decide if he was in any imminent danger.

"Yes. Do I know you?"

"No, you don't, Inspector." Clint said, "But we have a mutual acquaintance."

"And who might that be, mate?"

"Chief Inspector James Reed."

Frost suddenly relaxed.

"You're the American legend, then?" he asked. "The . . . what did he call you?"

"It doesn't matter," Clint said. "Just call me Clint and we'll get along fine."

"Adams," Frost said then. "Clint Adams."

"That's right."

The man shifted his suitcase to his left hand and held out his right.

"Just David Frost," he said, "not Inspector. Not on this side of the pond."

"Happy to meet you, David," Clint said, shaking the younger man's hand.

"Asked you to look out for me, did he?"

"Yes, he did."

"I guess he thinks I'll go off half-cocked and get myself in trouble."

"That he didn't say," Clint replied, "but there was only

so much he could put in a written message. Would you allow me to take you to a hotel?''

"Please do," Frost said. "I was going to rely on one of the drivers to recommend something, uh, affordable.''

"I have someplace in mind," Clint said. "In fact, I'm staying there now."

"Lead the way, then."

They walked to a cab and Clint told the driver, "You know where the Mayfair Hotel is?''

"Sure do."

"Take us there."

They got into the back of the cab and Clint closed the door behind them. He knocked on the top to indicate to the driver that they were ready to go, then settled back to enjoy the ride.

TWO

The Mayfair was a small but very good hotel on Thirty-eighth Street between Broadway and Seventh Avenue. Clint chose it because it was affordable, and centrally located. They could get to Central Park or Publisher's Row with equal alacrity.

As they alighted from the cab Frost looked up at the six-story hotel and nodded his approval.

Inside the Englishman registered, then agreed to meet Clint in the lobby in one hour for a bite to eat and a talk.

"I'm sure you're very interested in why I came," Frost said. "After all, if you're to be my baby-sitter you should know everything."

"Since you're a guest in my country," Clint said, "I'd rather think of myself as host."

Frost went to his room on the third floor, Clint to his own on the second.

An hour later Clint was waiting in the small, intimate lobby of the Mayfair when David Frost came down the stairs. He was dressed for a night out in London, long cape and top hat included.

"Have I overdressed?" he asked, noticing the way Clint was looking at him.

"Well," Clint said, "the hotel has a dining room. I thought we'd just go in there and get acquainted. Maybe later, though, we could go out. Of course, in that case I'd be underdressed."

Clint was wearing some of his best clothes, but compared to Frost he looked like a pauper.

"Perhaps tomorrow, you could help me find some clothing that is more appropriate," Frost suggested.

"We could do that, sure," Clint said. "How about dinner now?"

"Capital," Frost said, and they went into the dining room.

When Frost removed the hat and cape he seemed a little less formal and remote. The waiter offered to take both items and see to them, and Frost agreed.

"I'd like to eat something American," he told Clint.

"Nothing more American than a steak dinner," Clint said.

"Sounds fine."

"And coffee?"

"Actually, I'd prefer tea."

Clint ordered two steak dinners from the waiter, and asked him to bring coffee and tea right away.

"Yes, sir."

"Now then," Frost said as the waiter moved away, "perhaps I should tell you why I'm here."

"I'm listening."

"I'm tracking a killer," he said. "A madman who has killed six people in London."

"I thought you were here unofficially," Clint said.

"I am."

"So you're tracking him on your own?"

"Yes."

"What makes you think he's here?"

"My sources told me that he boarded a ship for America, and that New York City would be his first stop."

Clint decided not to ask the man about the validity of

his sources. After all, he'd already acted on the information and was here. "Do you know when he arrived?" he asked instead.

"No."

"Then he may be gone already," Clint said.

"Maybe," Frost said, "but I don't think so."

"Why not?"

"Because he was on the ship for a long time," Frost said, "and I don't believe he would have taken the chance of killing someone onboard. That means he's ready to kill again."

"Maybe he'd hold off until he got to another city—"

"No," Frost said, emphatically. "He won't be able to wait."

"You make it sound as if he has no choice."

"He doesn't," Frost said. "Believe me, he will kill before he leaves New York—if he has not already."

"Well," Clint said, "that should be easy enough to find out tomorrow. For tonight, though, I'd like to hear more about him, and why you've come all this way on your own to catch him."

The waiter came at that moment and served their coffee and tea.

"I will tell you what I know about him," Frost said, "which is not much. I am told he is rather average-looking, which makes it difficult to find him based on appearance. He's neither short nor tall, might have dark hair, but he might also wear hats to cover his hair color."

"How does he kill?"

"Ah," Frost said, "that I *can* tell you. He used his hands."

"No weapon?"

"No," Frost said. "He prefers to use his hands—he strangles his victims."

THREE

"He's strong," Frost said.

"How do you know that?" Clint asked.

"Because his third victim was a man, a very large, strong man."

"How many victims were men?"

"Three." Frost said. "Three men and three women."

"Well," Clint said, "at least he's not showing favorites."

"This steak is excellent," Frost commented.

"You'll forgive me for saying so, Inspector—"

"David, please," Frost said, "just David."

"All right, David. You, uh, seem very calm for a man who has tracked a killer across the Atlantic."

"Would you prefer hysterics?" Frost asked. "Histrionics?"

"Well, no, but—"

"Clint, I must keep my wits about me," Frost said, "or this madman will have me. You see, I believe he knows I will follow him."

"Now, how could he know that?" Clint scoffed.

"The same way I know he is somewhere in this vast city," the Englishman replied. "We feel each other."

Clint sat back and looked at the young man.

13

"Ah, yes, the Chief Inspector looked at me that very same way when I told him this."

"I'm sorry," Clint said, "I just—I didn't mean—"

"It's all right," Frost said. "It's just something I can't explain. Don't you have instincts about certain things?"

"Yes, I do."

"And your instincts have kept you alive?"

"They have because I've learned to listen to them," Clint said.

"Exactly!"

Clint held up a hand. "You don't have to explain any further. Instincts I understand."

"If he hasn't killed yet," Frost said, "he will. We must go to the local police and tell them."

"Ah," Clint said.

"What does that mean?"

"It means that *I* understand instincts," Clint said. "The police in this part of the world—and the country—believe in facts."

"Well, it's a fact that this man has killed six people in London. I've brought newspapers that can attest to that."

"That's good," Clint said, "but it won't prove to them that he's here."

"What do you suggest we do?"

"Let's check some back newspapers first. If he *has* killed already, the police here might welcome some help."

"And if he hasn't?

"I'm afraid they'll claim there's nothing for them to act on," Clint said.

"Until he actually does kill again?"

"Yes."

Frost looked down at the remains of his steak and set his fork aside.

"You have some strange customs in America, Clint."

"David," Clint said, "I'm afraid they're only going to get stranger for you."

FOUR

When Clint got back to his room he had company. Her name was Brenda Benet. They had met on the train and got better acquainted in the baggage car, since neither had a cabin. When they reached New York he discovered that she didn't have any hotel reservations, so they shared a cab to the Mayfair, and both got rooms.

Brenda, an actress, was coming to New York to be discovered. She wanted nothing as much as she wanted to be on the stage.

At the moment, though, she was in Clint's bed, where she wanted to be—where she had spent the night.

"Have you been back to your room yet?" he asked.

"No," she said. "I've been waiting for you."

"All day?"

She laughed and let go of the sheet. The laughter made her large breasts do interesting things. Brenda was short—barely five foot one—but she was full-bodied: busty and hippy, with a delicious butt that seemed ripe enough to squirt juices when he bit into it, which he'd done all night long.

Clint didn't have the heart to tell her that while her physical attributes made her a marvelous bed partner, he didn't think they were going to do much for her onstage—unless

15

she was just going to be scantily dressed and not try to do any acting, or singing.

Clint walked to the bed and sat down.

"Liar," he said.

"What?"

He leaned forward and smelled her, running his nose along her neck and shoulder until she shivered.

"You've had a bath."

"Okay, I lied," she said, smiling. "I did go out. I had a bath, went to see some people about getting onstage."

"What people?"

"Some names I knew," she said. "I heard Lillie Langtry was in town."

Clint knew Lillie very well.

"And was she?"

"No," she said. "I didn't find her. So I went to see some producers, contacts that someone in Denver gave me."

She had gotten on the train in Denver and switched trains in Chicago, which was where she and Clint had first met.

"And?" Clint prompted again.

"No luck," she said, "but I'm not giving up after one day."

"Good girl."

"I'm hungry," she said. "Can we have dinner?"

Clint debated whether or not to tell her he'd already had dinner. He decided to try to get around it without actually telling her, or lying.

"Why don't I arrange," he said, sliding his hand beneath the sheet, "to have some food sent up here . . . later?"

As he said "later," he slid his hand down into her tangle of pubic hair and stroked her.

"Oooh," she said, shivering and opening her legs, "much later."

She let her head fall back; her hands were behind her, flat on the mattress. He stroked her with his middle finger until she began to get wet and then slid his finger inside of her.

"Oh, God," she said, letting herself fall onto her back.

Clint removed his finger from her and brought it to his mouth. He licked it while she watched, and she bit her lips and said, "Jesus, that's so sexy. I never saw a man do that."

"It's just a taste," he said. "Now I want the main course."

He slid the sheet off of her and stared at her for a moment, all smooth skin and opulent curves. He kissed her breasts, touching the nipples lightly with his tongue, then kissed his way down her body, stopping briefly at her navel. Finally, still fully dressed, he was nestled between her legs, his mouth and tongue working avidly on her, savoring her scent and her sweet nectar.

"Oooh, yessss," she hissed, arching her back as he slipped his tongue into her. He slid his hands beneath her to cup her buttocks and lift her so he could get to her better. She cried out as he lapped at her, sipping her juices, licking the length of her moist slit and then finding her stiff little clit and lashing at it with his tongue until he felt her body go tense—as tense as the string on a bow just before the arrow is let fly—and then . . .

FIVE

He took to the streets after midnight.

This was his time, because it was their time. This was when the fornicators were out in force, prowling the streets, hawking their wares, flaunting their filth. He gathered his cape around him tightly and went in search of them.

It did not take him long to find the right place. The street was called Broadway, and it was alive at this time of the night. The gaslights were high on this street. Here he knew he would find them. The givers, the takers, the buyers, the sellers, the fallen angels and the sinners—men and women whose only thought was to spread their dirt and disease to the unsuspecting. Well, they would find out tonight that those days were over. The entire city would find out tonight what London already knew.

The sinners would die.

SIX

Clint woke the next morning with Brenda lying on his left arm. He slid from beneath her and quit the bed without waking her. He also wanted to dress without waking her and get out of the room. He knew if she woke up and he watched her stretch her naked body he probably wouldn't leave the room for hours.

He made it into the hall, fully clothed, closing and locking the door behind him without rousing her. He hurried down the hall and descended the steps to the lobby. Only then did he feel safe from the lure of her charms.

She was young, energetic, inventive, uninhibited—all the things he feared would lead him to an early grave if he tried to keep up with her.

He went to the dining room for breakfast and saw David Frost, already indulging.

Frost saw him and vigorously waved him over. As Clint approached, he saw that the man had bacon, eggs, spuds, biscuits, flapjacks, coffee, everything that made up an American—well, *several* American breakfasts.

"Come, sit." Frost spread his arms. "Eat with me."

Clint sat opposite the man, saying, "You look like you're fortifying yourself for a full day."

"I woke feeling invigorated and hungry," Frost told him.

"Did you meet a woman?" Clint joked.

"I have no time for women, Clint," Frost said. "Remember why I'm here."

"I do remember, David."

The waiter came over and Clint gave him his order: steak and eggs, plenty of coffee.

"More steak?" Frost asked. "For breakfast?"

"I had a long night, and I need the nourishment," Clint explained. "Especially if I'm going to try to keep up with you today."

"Then you are still going to help me?"

"I am," Clint said. "We'll check the newspapers first, and then I have some contacts we can talk to."

"Contacts? With the underworld?"

"Close, but not quite," Clint said. "I know some writers, some newspapermen, some policemen, who might be able to tell us something."

"Excellent!" Frost said. "Eat up, then, and let's get to it."

Frost bent to the task of consuming his own breakfast while Clint waited for the waiter to bring his. It struck him that Frost had both the youth and energy it would take to keep up with a Brenda Benet. Maybe he'd introduce them. She'd certainly test the man's resolve about not having time for women.

SEVEN

Clint took Frost to the offices of the *New York American*, down to their morgue files in the basement, where all the old newspapers were kept.

"We are not talking about something very old," Frost told the attendant. "Perhaps two or three weeks."

The old man squinted at Frost. "You ain't from around here, are you?"

"No, I am not. I'm from London."

"London, England?" the man asked, surprised.

"That's right. Do you know it?"

"I heard of it, but I ain't never been."

"Oh, well, you should go sometime. I think you would enjoy it very much."

"Ain't much chance of me gettin' out of here, let alone goin' to England," the old man said. "I'll get them papers for you."

"Thank you."

He brought the papers out and put them on a table for Clint and Frost, who spent hours going through them, page by page. Then they sat back and touched their faces, both of which were smudged with newsprint.

"Well," Frost said, "it would seem as if he hasn't struck yet."

23

"We could check some other newspaper, if you like,"
Clint offered.

"No," Frost replied, "I believe one is enough. If there
was a murder, it certainly would have made all the newspapers, wouldn't you agree?"

"Yes, I would."

As they were leaving, Frost gave the morgue man his
business card.

"If you to get to London, you must look me up."

The old man peered at the card and then asked, "Are
you really one of them Scotland Yard fellas?"

"Yes," Frost said, "I really am one of those Scotland
Yard fellows. Thank you for your help."

When Clint and Frost got outside they squinted at the sun-
light. They were standing on lower Broadway, very near
City Hall Park. Clustered around them were the offices of
the other New York newspapers, the *Daily*, the *Herald*, and
the *Evening Mail*.

"My God," Frost said, "and he spends all day in there.
Imagine what this must be like for him."

"I'll wager he doesn't come out until the sun has gone
down," Clint said.

"I'll not take that wager," Frost said, "as I am sure you
are correct."

"Are you hungry?" Clint asked.

"As a matter of fact," Frost answered, "I am quite fam-
ished."

"I know a place near here," Clint said.

"Lead on."

As they were sitting across from each other in the small
restaurant, Frost asked, "And are you armed now?"

"Yes, I am."

"But you're not wearing a holster."

"I've got a small gun tucked into my belt."

"And you carry a gun with you all the time?" Frost persisted. "Wherever you go?"

"Yes."

"And what about when you sleep?"

"There's always one within arm's reach."

"Even when you're with a woman?" Frost asked, with a glint in his eye that told Clint that maybe this apparently straitlaced Englishman did have a sense of humor, after all.

"Especially then."

"I say, that's a frightful way to have to live, isn't it?"

"It is," Clint said, "but I didn't choose it."

"Who would *choose* to live that way? I imagine, however, after years of having a reputation that you have little choice now."

"I have a choice," Clint said. "I can be seen walking down the street without a gun and die."

"Doesn't seem like much of a choice, does it?"

The waiter came over with two bowls of beef stew and some flaky biscuits.

"This is quite good," Frost commented after they had both tucked into their food.

"It's a specialty here."

They ate silently until about half their bowls were empty. Then Frost asked, "So now what?"

"Well, we can talk to some of those contacts I mentioned, but it doesn't seem like there's anything for them to know."

"Quite," Frost said. "I think I am now going to be reduced to simply waiting for him to strike."

"Strangulation murders are not a common thing hereabouts," Clint said. "If it happens, we'll hear about it."

The waiter had stopped to pour them some coffee and spoke when he set the pot down. "I couldn't help hearing you gents talking about murder."

"What about it?" Clint asked.

"Well . . . I was wondering if you heard what happened last night?"

"Hear what?" Clint asked.

"What happened?" Frost added.

"There was a murder last night not far from here, just off Broadway."

"Damn," Clint muttered.

"Who was murdered?" Frost asked anxiously. His intensity frightened the waiter, who backed away a few steps but, to his credit, didn't bolt.

"A girl," the man said. "A whore, from what I hear. Probably one of her johns did it."

"And how was she killed?" Frost asked.

"From what I heard," the waiter said, "she was strangled. Hey, 'scuse me, got another table. . . ."

EIGHT

"It's him," Frost said in the cab. "I know it's him."

After hearing the news they left the restaurant and went looking for a newspaper. They bought one, and then another, before realizing there was nothing being printed about the murder.

"Maybe the fellow was wrong," Frost suggested.

"Or maybe it happened too late or was discovered too early to make the newspapers," Clint said.

They decided that the only thing to do was to go to police headquarters and find out, so now they were in a cab on their way to Mulberry Street.

"Let's see what we can find out first—" Clint began, but Frost cut him off.

"No. It's him. I can *feel* it."

Clint didn't know what to do when the young man started talking like that, so they rode the rest of the way to police headquarters in silence.

The cab let them off in front of the building and they went inside, agreeing that Clint should do the talking. They presented themselves at the front desk and Clint asked for Detective Sergeant Egan, a police inspector he'd met on his last trip to New York. When he was told that the man was no longer with the department, he asked to talk to someone in charge.

"And what would he be in charge of?" the sergeant behind the desk asked.

"Sergeant, we understand that there was a murder committed last night. A young woman?"

The sergeant closed one eye. "And how would you be knowin' about that? It hasn't been in the papers yet."

"A waiter told us," Frost offered.

"Waiters and bartenders," the sergeant said. "They know everything, don't they?"

"Sergeant," Clint said, "we need to speak to whoever is handling the matter. We have some pertinent information."

"So, it's some pertinent information yer havin', eh?"

"That's right, Sergeant," Frost said. "Is there an inspector in charge?"

"You fellers wait right here," the man said. "I'll get you someone who's in charge."

"Thank you," Frost said.

After the man left, Clint said, "We'll have to find some way of convincing them you are who you say you are, since you have no credentials with you."

"Why lie?" Frost asked. "They'll believe me."

"We'll see . . ."

The sergeant returned with a rotund man in tow. He was wearing a three-piece suit and a bowler hat, and appeared to be in his late forties. He had a mustache and bushy muttonchops.

"Can I help you gents?" he asked. "My name is Inspector Jones." The man looked at the sergeant. "That'll be all, Callahan."

"Yes, sir."

"Inspector," Clint said, "my name is Clint Adams, and this is Inspector David Frost—"

"Inspector?" Jones asked, raising his eyebrows. "You're a policeman?"

"I am," Frost replied. "With Scotland Yard."

"Ah," Jones said, "that's very impressive, Inspector. I suppose you have identification to prove it?"

"No, I don't," Frost said.

"And why would that be?"

"Because I am in this country as a private citizen, Inspector," Frost said, "not as a policeman."

"I see." Jones looked at Clint. "I've heard of you, Adams. I suppose you can prove who you are?"

"If I have to, but we'd have to go back to my hotel to do it."

"Which hotel?"

"The Mayfair."

Jones regarded the two men for a few moments, then said, "Follow me back to my office. We'll continue to talk there."

NINE

"You asked for Sergeant Egan when you came in," Jones said, when he was settled behind his desk.

"That's right," Clint said.

"I know Egan."

"I was told he wasn't with the department anymore."

"That's correct," Jones said. "He's out West somewhere, with his wife, doing God knows what."

"I see."

"He told me about you, though, about the last time you were in New York. That whole Roosevelt thing."

"I remember."

"This was his office, as a matter of fact."

Clint looked around, then said, "No, I don't think so. His was smaller and, I think, down a different hall."

"So it was," Jones said.

"And he wasn't married."

"No, he wasn't," Jones agreed, "but he got married, and she wanted to go West."

"Ah . . ."

"All right, then," Jones said. "Tell me what you know about this murder."

"If I may speak . . ." Frost said.

"Go ahead."

31

"Was the victim strangled?"

"She was."

"Manually?"

"If you mean did he use his hands, the answer's yes. There are bruises on her throat to indicate that."

"And her neck?" Frost continued. "Was it broken?"

"Yes," Jones said, beginning to look interested. "By someone very strong. Say, you *do* know something about this, don't you?"

"Inspector," Frost said, "I have followed this man from England. He killed six people in London in exactly that same way—men *and* women. This would appear to be his first victim here—unless you've already had one before this?"

"No," Jones said, "this is the first one." The policeman looked at Clint. "He really is from Scotland Yard, isn't he?"

"Yes," Clint said, "he is. Arrived here just yesterday."

"And how do you know him?"

"I know the man he works for in England, Chief Inspector Reed. We met when I went to England for a gun expo several years ago."

"I see," Jones said thoughtfully. "All right, then, Inspector Frost, why don't you tell me everything you know about this strangler?"

Clint sat back and listened to Frost talk. It seemed the young Scotland Yard inspector knew a lot about what the strangler had done, but didn't know anything about the man himself.

"You say you had a contact who kept you apprised of his movements?" Jones asked when the Englishman was finished.

"That's right."

"And this contact told you the killer was coming to America?"

"Yes."

"But he never told you what the man looked like?"

"No," Frost admitted.

"Inspector," Jones said, "did it ever occur to you that your contact might actually be the killer?"

Frost sat forward in his chair and replied, "Yes, it did, Inspector Jones. In which case he virtually challenged me to come here and stop him."

"And you believe you're up to that challenge?"

"Yes, sir, I do . . . with your help."

"Oh, with *my* help?" Jones asked.

Clint didn't like the tone of the man's voice.

"Well, let me ask you something, Inspector," Jones continued.

Frost sat back. "Go ahead."

"You had a contact—maybe even the killer himself—and he still killed six people in London, and you couldn't catch him."

Frost did not reply, only stared at the man.

"What makes you think you can come over here, where you don't know anything or anyone, and catch him if you couldn't even catch him in your own country?"

"I'll tell you why," Frost said. "Because he and I know each other, we can *feel* each other. I know he's here because I can feel it."

"And because he killed a woman last night."

"I knew it before that," Frost said. "I knew it was only a matter of time before he struck."

Jones looked at Clint, who shrugged and said, "That's what he told me."

"Why didn't you come to me sooner?"

"He only arrived in the country last evening, Inspector," Clint said. "This was the earliest we could have gotten here, anyway."

"But first you had to go through some newspaper morgues, eh?"

"How did you know that?" Clint asked.

Jones pointed at their hands and said, "That newsprint ink is hard to get off, isn't it?"

Both men looked down: Their fingertips were still black from the stuff.

"After all," Jones said, "I am a detective." He stood up abruptly. "All right, gentlemen, thank you for coming in. If I can think of any way you can help, I'll call on you."

Clint and Frost exchanged a glance, then stood as well.

"I am also staying at the Mayfair, Inspector," Frost said.

"Good," Jones said, "that'll make it easy to find the both of you."

"Am I to assume, then, that we'll work together?" Frost asked.

Jones gave him a humorless smile. "I'll let you know when I need you, Inspector."

TEN

Clint and Frost hailed a cab and told the driver to take them to the Mayfair Hotel. They sat in silence for a while, before Frost broke it.

"He didn't believe me."

"He did," Clint said. "He just doesn't think you'll be much help here."

"He's a fool, then," Frost said. "No one knows this killer like I do."

"To be honest, David, it doesn't sound like you know him very well at all."

"Is that a fact?" Frost asked. "Well, what would you say if I told you I could predict when he will strike again, and where?"

"And who?"

"Not exactly," Frost said, "but it will be a woman, if he follows his pattern."

"When?"

"Three days' time."

"And the where?"

"Somewhere near a theater."

"The theater district?" Clint said. "That would be Broadway. Why didn't you tell Inspector Jones?"

"I didn't think he'd believe me," Frost said.

"And if he did he'd tell you to stay away."

"Precisely."

"So what do you plan to do?"

"Be there when he strikes."

"On Broadway?"

"Wherever."

"You can't cover all that ground alone," Clint said.

"I don't intend to," Frost said. "You're going to help me."

Clint looked out the window of the carriage. "I was afraid you were going to say something like that."

By the time they reached the hotel, Clint had not only agreed to help Frost, he'd also agreed to bring in some others to help.

"Hopefully," he said, as they stepped away from the cab, "the two men I have in mind are still in New York."

"And who are they?"

"Their names are Delvecchio and Anson Eickhorst."

"Those are their names? Any first name for this Delvecchio?"

"Not that I'm aware of."

"And who are they?" Frost repeated.

"Delveccio is a private detective, and as such I should be able to locate him if he's in the city," Clint replied.

"And the other?"

"A lawyer."

"A barrister?"

"Yes, but nonpracticing. He does other things to make ends meet."

"Like what?"

"Like hiring out as a bodyguard," Clint said. "That's what he and Delvecchio were doing the last time he was in New York, guarding the body of a young politician named Theodore Roosevelt."

"How long will it take you to locate them?" Frost asked as they entered the hotel lobby.

"I should be able to find Delvecchio today," Clint said. "He'll have to find Eickhorst—hopefully in the next three days."

"Can the four of us cover this Broadway area you're speaking of?"

"Probably not," Clint said, "but four of us can sure do it better than two can."

"You have a point."

"Meantime, Inspector, I suggest that you stay inside and make yourself scarce until I find them."

"And why is that?"

"Does your killer know what you look like?"

"I'm sure he does," Frost said. "I'm sure he's watched me at the scenes of his crime, laughing at me all the while."

"Well, then, you don't want to run into him, do you? He'll know you and you won't know him. That won't bode well for you, will it?"

"You have a point," Frost allowed.

"Stay in the hotel today, take your dinner here, and I'll be back when I have some news."

"It goes against everything I believe in to cower here—"

"You're not cowering."

"All right, then, hiding. It goes against everything for me to hide here while he's out there, finding his next victim."

"By the way," Clint said, "you said his next victim would be a woman?"

"That's right."

"But you didn't say what sort of woman she'd be," Clint said. "Are we, uh, talking about a prostitute?"

"No, my dear fellow," Frost said, "we are talking about an actress—preferably a young one."

ELEVEN

When Clint was last in New York, Delvecchio was doing business across the new Brooklyn Bridge from Manhattan. In order to find out just where Delvecchio's office was, Clint went down to Wall Street to see Teddy Roosevelt, Sr. It was actually the senior Roosevelt they had been guarding, even though it appeared that the junior one was going to go down in history as a great man—in Clint's humble opinion. He had not seen the young Teddy since the business at Little Misery, in Missouri.

Teddy, Sr., was happy to see Clint and welcomed him into his office. Clint had to turn down drinks and dinner before he could get right to business. There wasn't much time to waste. After he explained the situation to Roosevelt, the man supplied him with Delvecchio's address in Brooklyn. It seemed that the detective had been doing other jobs for the banker since the last time.

Clint thanked Roosevelt, left the building, and got a cab to Brooklyn.

Brooklyn was not as well-to-do as Manhattan, did not have the large buildings, nor the busy streets that its neighboring borough had. The cab dropped Clint in front of a three-

story building. According to Roosevelt, Delvecchio had
rooms here and conducted his business from them.

Clint found the right door and knocked. He heard boot
heels on a wooden floor as someone approached the door.
When it opened he found himself looking at the man he
knew only as Delvecchio.

"Well, I'll be damned," the detective said. "I'll be double damned."

"It's not that bad," Clint said.

"What the hell is Clint Adams doing in Brooklyn?"

"If you let me in," Clint said, "I'll tell you."

Delvecchio extended his hand to be shaken and then
pulled Clint into the room.

"This calls for a drink," he said. "I've got a bottle of
whiskey in my desk drawer."

"Just the bottle?"

"And two glasses."

"Just one drink," Clint said, "and then you and I have
business to discuss."

"More work for me?" Delvecchio asked. "Last time
wasn't exciting enough for you?"

"This time will be pretty exciting, Del," Clint said.
"Guaranteed."

Delvecchio fetched the bottle and glasses and poured two
fingers of whiskey into each. He handed Clint a glass and
clinked his against it.

"To old friends and comrades."

They drank.

"Speaking of which," Clint said, handing the glass back,
"I'll be needing our friend Anson, as well. Is he still
around?"

"Still around, yep."

"Practicing law?"

"Ah, no," Delvecchio said, "he hasn't gotten his license
back yet. He's still doing, uh, odd jobs."

"Well," Clint said, "this one will be pretty odd."

He watched the younger man stow away the bottle and

the two glasses—without wiping the glasses out. He decided to remember that the next time the detective offered him a drink.

"All right," Delvecchio said. "The drinks are done, the bottle and glasses are put away. I'll have a seat behind my desk and we'll do business."

He pulled his chair over and sat down, beckoning Clint to sit opposite him.

"All right, Clint," he said, lacing his fingers behind his head and putting his feet up on the desk, "I'm all ears."

TWELVE

Delvecchio listened silently and intently while Clint told him about the murders in London, and the possibility that the murderer was here in New York, closely pursued by a Scotland Yard man.

"I've heard of Scotland Yard," Delvecchio said when Clint was finished, "but I didn't think it really existed."

"It does," Clint said, "and Inspector Frost is here in New York to prove it."

"Well, from what you say he's here to do more than that."

"That's right. He's here to catch the bastard."

"And how did you get involved?"

Clint told Delvecchio about how he'd met Chief Inspector James Reed.

"And he asked you to baby-sit?" Delvecchio wanted to know.

"He asked me to help," Clint clarified, "and now I'm asking you."

"Whoa, wait a minute," Delvecchio said. He dropped his feet to the floor and held out his hands in a "stop" motion. "Hold on. This sounds like a favor, like something I'm not getting paid for."

43

"And they say you're dumb," Clint said, shaking his head.

Delvecchio agreed to approach Eickhorst about the job, although—as he said—"Job implies that one is getting paid for it."

"Look," Clint said, "if you guys want to get paid I'll put up the—"

"Easy, take it easy," Delvecchio said, cutting him off. "We owe you. Don't worry about paying."

"You owe me for what?"

"You introduced us to a better class of people to work for," Delvecchio said. "Both Eickhorst and I are doing better because of you. We did some more work for Roosevelt, Senior, and he's recommended us to other bigwigs, as well. So don't worry, I'm just kidding around with you. We'll be there when you want us."

"How about tomorrow morning, at my hotel?" Clint suggested. "The least I can do is buy breakfast, and then I'll introduce you to the inspector."

"We'll be there," Delvecchio said.

"You can speak for Eickhorst?"

"Oh, sure," the detective said. "See, we're kind of partners now."

"Partners."

"Right. We'll be there."

Delvecchio walked Clint to the door.

"It's good to see you, Clint. Have you heard form Junior, lately?"

"Not since I saw him in Missouri some time ago," Clint said.

"He's gonna be a big man in this country," Delvecchio said. "It's written all over him."

"I agree."

The two men shook hands and Clint made his way back downstairs to find a cab.

•   •   •

It took a while for him to find a driver that wanted to take him to Manhattan, and in the end he had to offer the man far more than the fair price would have been. Clint wondered if this was a practice that went on between Brooklyn and Manhattan. If it was, he doubted that people would put up with it for very long.

When he got back to the hotel, he went to David Frost's door and knocked. He frowned and knocked again, in case the man was asleep. When there was still no answer he tried the door and found it locked.

"Damn it," he said. The man had gone out, after the talk they'd had about lying low.

Well, Clint thought, he was all grown up, and if he wanted to get himself killed that was his choice.

THIRTEEN

But, of course, he couldn't leave it at that. He went down to the lobby and checked the dining room. When he didn't see Frost in there he went to the front desk.

"Are there any messages for me?" he asked the clerk.

"No, sir, Mr. Adams, no messages."

"Did you see my friend leave?" he asked. "The Englishman?"

"Mr. Frost? Why, yes, sir, I did. He left about three hours ago."

"Did he say where he was going? Or when he would be back?"

"No, sir."

"Okay, thanks," Clint said.

"Uh, he did ask me a question, though."

"Oh? What was that?"

"He asked me where the closest place was to buy a gun," the clerk said.

"Well," Clint said, "why don't you tell me what you told him. . . ."

The clerk had sent Frost to a gun shop on Chambers Street, which wasn't far from City Hall. He admitted that the shop belonged to his brother-in-law, and he was always trying to send some business his way. "No harm in that," Clint told him, and left.

• • •

The gun shop was one of many little stores on Chambers Street. Clint entered and immediately smelled dust and gun oil. He hoped that the proprietor at least kept the dust away from the gun oil.

"Can I help you, sir?" the man behind the desk asked. He was tall and balding, with close-set eyes and a weak chin. He smiled when he asked the question and it was not a pretty sight. Caring for his teeth obviously was not one of this man's major concerns.

"I'm looking for a friend of mine," Clint said. "He was sent here by your brother-in-law."

"Lucas," the man said. "He sends a lot of business my way. Who would your friend be?"

"I think you'd remember him," Clint said. "He's an Englishman."

"Oh, him," the man said. "Yeah, he was here."

"Did you sell him a gun?"

"I did. I tried to sell him something new, but he wouldn't, uh, bite."

"So you sold him something old?"

"A Navy Colt. He said he didn't have much money, so . . ."

Navy Colts were not only old, they were big.

"Did it work?" he asked.

"Of course," the man said indignantly. "I wouldn't sell a man a gun that didn't fire."

"Uh-huh."

"In fact, he went out back and fired it a few times, just to make sure. I got a bit of a range back there."

Well, at least the Englishman was that smart, Clint thought. "And it fired?" he said aloud.

"Like a dream."

"Right."

"I'll tell you one thing, though."

"What?"

"That feller couldn't hit the side of a barn if he was standing inside of it."

"Bad shot, huh?"

"The worst! I ain't never seen a man shoot that bad, and I seen a lot of 'em," the man assured Clint.

"I see."

"Can I ask you something?"

"Sure."

"What good's a gun to somebody who can't shoot?"

"You know," Clint said, "I'll ask him that when I find him."

FOURTEEN

Clint left the gun shop and stopped just outside, hands on his hips. Where would Frost have gone after he bought the gun? Down to the area of Broadway that had the concert saloons and theaters, to check it out? The man had an hour's head start on him, so Clint decided the best thing to do was go back to the hotel and wait for him there.

He was sitting in the lobby waiting for Frost when Brenda Benet came walking in, looking dejected.

"Well, hello," she said, when she saw him. "Waiting for me?"

"I wish I could say I was," he said. "I'm waiting for a friend."

She came over and sat next to him on the sofa.

"I've had a very frustrating day."

"Couldn't find any jobs?"

"If I wanted a job I could find one easy," she said. "There's plenty of openings for waitresses out there. Unfortunately, I want a career."

"And no luck, huh?"

"Not today," she said, "but there's always tomorrow. Will I see you later, after you finish with your friend?"

"I don't know, Brenda," Clint replied. "I can't say for—

wait a minute. Here he comes now. I'll introduce you.''

She turned and saw Frost walking toward them.

"Oh, my," she said. "He's very handsome."

"I guess he is." At that moment Clint didn't care how handsome the man was. He just wanted to wring his neck.

He stood as Frost approached them. The Englishman was about to say something when he noticed Brenda standing next to Clint.

"Oh, hello," he said to her.

"Hello."

"David Frost," Clint said, "this is Brenda Benet. Brenda, Inspector Frost of Scotland Yard."

"How nice to meet you," she said, putting out her hand. Frost took the hand and raised it to his lips.

"I'm very pleased to meet such a charming young lady," he said.

"Oh, my . . ." she said. "What a lovely accent."

"Why, thank you."

"Well," she said, "you two have business. I hope to see you again, Mist—I mean, Inspector."

"Please," Frost said, "just call me David."

Frost might have said that women weren't an interest of his while he was tracking his killer, but the man's eyes actually looked hungry as they roamed over her body. Both men watched her walk to the steps and go up.

"Who is that lovely creature?" Frost asked.

"Just a girl I met on the train," Clint said.

"I see," Frost said. "Are you and she . . ."

"We're friends," Clint said. "David, I thought we agreed you wouldn't go out."

"Ah, you're upset with me. I can't say I blame you, but allow me to explain."

"Go ahead."

"I started to feel like a sitting duck here, Clint. I simply felt the need to go out and get myself some protection."

"A Navy Colt?" Clint asked. "Jesus, we could have

STRANGLER'S VENDETTA 53

gotten you something better than that. The way you've got it tucked into your pants, it looks like you're going to lose them."

Frost looked down at himself and chuckled.

"Yes, I suppose it's looks a bit ridiculous, doesn't it?"

"I went to the gun shop where you bought it, looking for you."

"Did he tell you how dismally I shoot?"

"Yes."

"Well," Frost said, "I really bought it to use close-up."

"Oh? You want to put a hole that big in the killer? Why not get a cannon?"

"I want to kill him, Clint," Frost said. "I'm really not concerned with how large a hole it takes to do it."

"Well, for one thing, you can't go walking around New York with a huge gun like that. I hope you didn't pay a lot for it."

Frost told him how much he'd spent.

"You paid too much."

"It's all right," Frost said. "I'll keep it in my room."

"I'll get you something more appropriate," Clint said, "and show you how to use it."

"Thank you," Frost said. "I shall find it very interesting to learn how to use a gun from you."

"We can get started tomorrow."

"What about your two men?"

"They'll be here tomorrow for breakfast," Clint said. "You can meet them then."

"I'll look forward to it."

"How about a drink?" Clint asked.

"I think I'll just go to my room. I'm quite tired, for some reason."

"All right," Clint said. "Meet me down here at eight for breakfast."

"I will be here," Frost said. "Good night. I'm . . . sorry about the gun."

"Don't worry about it," Clint said. "Good night."

He watched as the Englishman walked up the stairs, moving as if he truly were exhausted, and then turned and went into the bar.

FIFTEEN

When Brenda didn't come to his room that night Clint wasn't surprised. He had seen the way she and Frost had looked at each other, and he *was* handsome and closer to her own age. Clint wasn't disappointed, either. They had enjoyed each other's company for a brief time, and now it was time to move on.

When Frost came down to the lobby the next morning he didn't look as well-rested as he might have.

"Good morning," he greeted Clint.

"Morning."

"Are they here yet?"

"No," Clint said, "but they'll be here. Let's go into the dining room and get a table."

"All right.

They went in and got a table for four. By the time the coffee was delivered to the table both Delvecchio and Eickhorst had entered the dining room. Since Clint was seated so he could see the entire room, he spotted them right away.

"They're here," he said, and waved the two men over.

Frost looked over his shoulder, then stood as the two men approached the table.

"Inspector Frost of Scotland Yard," Clint said, "meet Delvecchio . . ."

The two men shook hands and looked each other over.

". . . and Anson Eickhorst."

Eickhorst was a white-haired man who could have been thirty or forty, maybe even older—or younger if the white hair was premature. He had the kind of face that could go either way.

After Eickhorst shook hands with Frost, he extended his hand to Clint and shook his warmly.

"Good to see you again."

"You, too, Anson. Come on, boys, have a seat and some breakfast."

When all four were seated the waiter came over and took their orders.

"How much has Del told you, Anson??" Clint asked.

"Enough."

"Are you in or out?"

"I'm here, ain't I?" the man answered. "I didn't come just for some breakfast."

"Del?"

"I'm here," Delvecchio said. "Always interested in taking a killer off the streets—even though I think it's the police's job."

"So do I," Frost said. "We're just going to help them a little."

"How little?" Delvecchio asked.

"And how?" Eickhorst added.

"Inspector Frost has followed this killer here from England," Clint explained. "He feels he knows him very well. I'll let him tell it."

"Thank you, Clint," Frost said. "I believe he will follow the same pattern he followed in London, gentlemen. There he killed a man, and then a woman—an actress, actually."

"He's killed a man already?" Eickhorst asked.

"Yes," Frost said, "last night. He strangled him."

"Man's got to be strong to strangle another man," Delvecchio said.

"He is strong," Frost said, "very strong."

"So then we're looking for a big, strong man," Delvecchio said.

"Not necessarily," the Englishman disagreed. "All the information we had in London indicated he was a medium-size man."

"With strong hands," Clint said.

"Right."

"So where do you think he's going to show up next?" Delvecchio asked.

"Someplace where there are theaters," Frost said. "Lots of theaters."

"Broadway," Delvecchio said.

"That is what Clint suggested, yes," Frost said, "and I concur."

"And when is this next killing supposed to take place?" Delvecchio continued grilling the Englishman.

"If he stays with his pattern," Frost replied, "three nights from today."

"And we're supposed to go to Broadway and just wait for him?" the detective scoffed.

"And we don't know what he looks like?" Eickhorst finally spoke up.

"That's correct," Frost said.

Delvecchio looked at Clint.

"Well, I'm sure glad your friend here doesn't want us to do something hard."

"Just watch the women," Frost said. "The attractive women. He will pick a pretty one."

"Well," Delvecchio said, "that doesn't sound like a hardship, standing around watching the pretty women walk around Broadway."

"Don't watch the prostitutes, though," Frost warned.

"He doesn't like whores?" Eickhorst asked.

"No, he doesn't," Frost said, and then added, "Not yet, anyway."

SIXTEEN

They made arrangements for Delvecchio and Eickhorst to return to the hotel in two days' time, in the morning.

"We'll want to get the jump on him, as you Americans say," Frost said. "Find our positions along Broadway."

"We'll have to parcel it out," Delvecchio said. "There's a lot of ground to cover."

"Mr. Delvecchio, why don't you do that?" Frost asked. "You seem to have a knowledge of the area in question."

"I know it very well, Inspector," Delvecchio said. "I'd be happy to take care of that."

After breakfast they all shook hands; Delvecchio and Eickhorst left. Clint and Frost remained at the table and had another pot of coffee.

"They seem . . . competent," Frost said.

"They're both very capable men," Clint assured him. "You can count on them to be there when you need them."

"I imagine there is little else to ask for."

"Do you want to work with a gun today?" Clint asked. "We can go back to that gun shop on Chambers Street, exchange the Navy Colt for a proper weapon, and use the shop's range."

"That sounds good, but . . . there is something I need to discuss with you."

"Oh?"

"Yes," Frost said, looking suddenly uncomfortable, "something I'm feeling very badly about. Guilty, you might say, and I feel I have to—"

"Did Brenda come to your room last night?"

Frost looked at Clint in total surprise.

"Why, yes . . . how did you know? Did you see her? I really didn't think—"

"No, I didn't see her, but I saw the way the two of you looked at each other in the lobby. It doesn't surprise me."

"And you don't mind?"

"No," Clint said, "I don't mind at all."

"But . . . I thought you and she . . ."

"We were, and we did, but not any more," Clint said. "Enjoy yourself with her, Inspector. You deserve some time for yourself."

"Well . . . I really hadn't thought about that," Frost said.

"Well, maybe you should. Do you want to go up and talk to her, or can we go to the gun shop?"

"No, no," Frost said, "business first. By all means, let us go to the gun shop."

SEVENTEEN

The owner was glad to exchange the Navy Colt for something more manageable for the Englishman, a .32 Colt Paterson.

"Fits your hand better, doesn't it?" Clint asked. They were behind the shop in a makeshift outdoor firing range.

"Indeed," Frost said, hefting it, flexing his hand around it.

"Let me see you fire it."

"At what?"

There was a bull's-eye target set up at the end of the range, which was only about fifty feet from where they were standing.

"See how close you can come to the bull's-eye."

Frost raised the gun, closed one eye, and fired. He missed the target completely.

"Keep both of your eyes open," Clint instructed. "Don't 'aim' the gun, just point it—and squeeze the trigger, don't jerk it. Got it?"

"I've got it."

This time the Englishman lifted the gun and kept both eyes open. Clint could see that he followed directions well. He was pointing the gun, not aiming it, and then he gently squeezed the trigger. The very edge of the target jumped as the bullet just barely touched it.

"I hit it that time," Frost said.

"Just barely," Clint retor. "Let's try it again."

They did, and again . . . and again . . . and again, until Frost was consistantly hitting the target. Nothing near the bull's-eye, but he *was* hitting the target.

"If you're going to shoot at a man, you want to pick the biggest target." Clint touched his own torso and said, "That would be here. If you just try to wound a man, he's liable to kill you instead."

"A wound is not what I'm looking for," Frost said.

They went back into the shop and bought some extra rounds of ammunition.

"I'm giving you a discount because my brother-in-law sent you," the owner said.

"That's great," Clint said, doubting that they were getting any kind of discount at all. "Thanks."

They left the shop, Frost with the Colt Paterson tucked into his belt, his jacket covering it.

"Next," Clint said, "some American-style clothes."

"Excellent," Frost said. "I do not want to stand out when we are on Broadway."

"Believe me," Clint said, "you won't."

They got back to the hotel, Frost carrying several packages of jeans and shirts and an American-style suit he'd insisted on buying.

In the lobby Clint said, "You spent a lot of money on clothes. I was thinking one shirt and one pair of jeans."

"One can never have too much clothes."

"But the money," Clint said. "If Scotland Yard isn't backing you, then you're using your own money."

"I took my life's savings out of the bank," Frost said. "It should last me a while longer."

"You want this guy badly enough to leave yourself penniless when it's over?"

"I want him that bad," Frost replied. "Besides, my job is waiting for me when I get back."

"I see."

"Have you ever wanted anything that badly? That you'd spend your last dime and your last ounce of breath to get it?"

Clint thought a moment. "Yeah, once or twice."

"Ah, then you understand."

"I suppose I do," Clint said.

"I am going to go up and try on some of my new clothes," Frost said.

"I'll be having a drink," Clint said. "Come in when you're ready."

"You won't recognize me," Frost assured him, and went upstairs.

Clint doubted that the new clothes would make *that* much of a difference.

EIGHTEEN

He was wrong.

When Frost walked into the bar, Clint saw him from his back table and, for a moment, didn't recognize him. Then he caught the newness of the clothing the man was wearing and gave him a closer look.

"Son of a bitch," he said, as Frost sat down opposite him. "I didn't recognize you."

"Thank you," Frost said. "I was hoping you would say that."

"Let's just hope the killer can't recognize you, either."

"It hardly matters."

"Why?"

"He knows I'm here."

"How can he—oh, you mean he feels that you're here?" Clint asked.

"Yes."

Clint scratched his head.

"So what if he decides not to follow the same pattern as he did in London? What if he decides to leave, rather than take a chance on you catching him?"

"You don't understand," Frost said. "He *wants* me to catch him."

"What?"

"That's the game, you see," Frost went on. "To see how long and how far he can go before I catch him. He won't leave New York until he's established his pattern."

"You're sure of that."

"I'm dead sure."

"That's not a phrase I want to hear right now," Clint said.

Watching Adams and Frost made the killer smile, but he hid it behind his hand. Of course he would establish his pattern and, by doing so, his superiority over them. It didn't matter how many men they had on Broadway in two days' time: He would accomplish his mission and go on from there.

Six bodies, and then he would move on—unless he could be caught by then.

Sometimes he felt very tired and *wished* that he would be caught. A jail cell would be very restful.

But he didn't relish the thought of dancing on the end of a rope.

Not at all.

NINETEEN

There was little to do over the next, full day but wait.

"What if he decides to strike earlier?" Clint asked. They were in the hotel's bar, enjoying an after-dinner beer.

"He won't."

"Why not?"

"That would break the pattern," Frost said, "and he won't—and can't—do that."

"You sound more like a doctor than a policeman, Inspector."

"I understand the criminal mind," Frost said. "That is what makes me a good policeman. This killer has to prove himself better than me. That is why he will follow the same pattern, to—how do you say it here?—to show me up?"

"Yes," Clint said, "to show you up."

They left the bar and stepped into the lobby.

"I think I'll go to my room," Frost said.

"Somebody waiting there for you?"

"I don't know, actually," Frost said. "I was just thinking about getting some rest and reading a book. Something by your Mark Twain."

Clint wondered if he should return the favor and go out to find something by Dickens.

"All right, Inspector," he said, "I'll see you in the morning."

Frost started away, then turned back.

"Of course there's always another alternative."

"And what would that be in this case?"

"He could decide to go ahead and break the pattern, and set up a new one."

"In which case we're out of luck."

"Well," Frost said, "*somebody* would be out of luck—like his next victim."

With that the Inspector turned and walked to the stairs, taking them to the second and then the third floor, and his room.

Clint decided to go out and get some of the evening air. He figured to simply walk around the block and come right back, but he had only gone halfway when he heard the shot, and the impact of the lead slug on the wall of the building.

Even before the sound of the ricochet faded, he was down on one knee with his Colt New Line out. Unlike his regular Colt, or even Frost's Colt Paterson, the New Line really was for close-up work.

He waited, and waited some more, and when no further shots came he slowly stood up. Either the shooter had out-waited him or he had become impatient and had given up. The latter seemed to be the case.

Clint tucked the New Line in his pants at the small of his back and took a deep breath. One shot only. Maybe that was all the man had time—or the guts—for. In any case, it wasn't enough for Clint to pinpoint where the shot had come from.

He checked the gouge mark on the building and surmised that the bullet was a large caliber. If it had hit him, it would have done major damage. How had the shooter done so well in the dark? he wondered.

He decided to go back the way he had come. No telling who was waiting ahead.

Clint had been shot at before, many times. Usually it was

because somebody recognized him and wanted to claim they killed the Gunsmith. However, this time he had to wonder if Frost's killer had taken the shot. If he were watching the inspector from England, then he knew that Clint was helping him. Maybe he was trying to reduce the contest to one against one. Hopefully, he didn't know that the odds had become four against one.

Clint got back to the hotel without any more shots being fired. He went and had a drink before he returned to his room.

Once there, he hung his gun belt on the bedpost, made sure the window was locked, did the same to the door, then kicked off his boots and reclined on the bed. Would whoever wanted him dead try again tonight? Or had that been just a warning shot?

Of course, the killer was a stranger, but that didn't mean he *didn't* have a gun.

Did it?

Inspector David Frost looked out the window of his room to the street down below. He saw Clint Adams return from his walk.

"David . . ." Brenda called.

Frost turned and looked at her. She was kneeling in the center of the bed, naked. He took in the sight of her, all butt and breasts, this girl, solidly built, perfect for loving.

"Come back to bed," she said. "We're not finished."

The girl was insatiable—but that was okay because Frost had a lot of excess energy he wanted to work off. He wanted to be very calm when the time came to go down to Broadway.

He turned, also naked, and as he stared at her his penis began to rise to the occasion.

"Oh, my," she said, staring at him, "you are such a beautiful man."

He walked to the bed, and she slithered to the end of it

so they could kiss. She reached between them and stroked
his erection with one hand, cradling his balls with the other.
Then she slid off the bed, got on her knees on the floor,
and slid the length of him into her hot, wet mouth.

TWENTY

The next morning Clint was having breakfast alone when he looked up and saw Inspector Jones enter the dining room. He watched the man for a few moments, instinctively knowing that the policeman was looking for him. He didn't help the man, just let him scan the room until he spotted him and came over.

"The desk clerk told me you were in here," Jones said. "Mind if I sit?"

"Sit, and have coffee," Clint said.

"Thanks."

There was already a second cup on the table, so Clint filled it for him.

"What can I do for you today, Inspector?"

Jones sipped the coffee and put the cup down.

"I think I was a little . . . harsh when we last spoke," he said.

"Oh? In what way?"

"I realize you and your Scotland Yard friend were offering to help, and I didn't accept the offer in the spirit that it was given."

This sounded to Clint like a prepared speech.

"So now you want our help?"

"There was a shot fired near here last night," Jones said.

71

"Really? Is that unusual, a shot being fired?" Clint asked.

"In New York it is." Jones replied. "Especially at that time of night. Would you happen to know anything about it?"

"As a matter of fact, I do," Clint said. "I was taking a walk when someone fired a shot at me out behind the hotel."

"Did you see who it was?"

"No. There was only one shot, and I didn't have time to find the muzzle flash."

"Do you think this is in connection with this killer Inspector Frost is chasing?"

"Could be," he conceded. "Could also be somebody just recognized me and decided to take a chance and see if they could make a reputation for themselves."

"I guess that's happened before."

"A lot of times."

Jones sipped his coffee and stared into the cup for a few moments.

"I had a talk with Theodore Roosevelt, Senior," he said, finally.

"About what?"

"About you," Jones said. "He speaks very highly of you."

"That's nice."

"I . . . I'm familiar with your reputation, of course, but I needed something more than that."

"Well, I hope Mr. Roosevelt gave you what you needed," Clint replied.

"He did . . . and now I need for you to give me something."

"Which is?"

"Information on this Scotland Yard inspector."

"To be honest, Inspector, I don't know much about him. I was asked by a friend to try to help him. All I know is what I've learned since his arrival."

"And what's that?"

"That he's dedicated to catching this killer. In fact, you might say he was obsessed."

"I don't like obsessed people," Jones said. "They make too many mistakes."

"Do they?"

"Yes, they do."

"Well, maybe I can keep him from making them."

"Do you two have any . . . plans to catch this killer?" Jones asked.

"We're . . . still discussing it," Clint said evasively.

"Well, if you do decide to do something, let me in on it, will you?"

"Sure, Inspector," Clint said. "We'll keep the local police informed about everything we do."

Jones studied Clint for a moment, suspecting sarcasm, then stood up and said, "Have a good day," and left.

What, Clint wondered, was *that* all about?

TWENTY-ONE

Clint decided to take Frost down to the theater district, even though Delvecchio was going to figure out the placing for the four men. He just wanted to show the man what it looked like.

In the cab on the way, Clint told Frost about being shot at the night before.

"And you didn't see who it was?"

"No," Clint said, "and I didn't see where the shot came from."

"You don't seem . . . disturbed about being shot at," Frost said.

"Oh, I'm disturbed, all right," Clint said, "but it happens to me a lot. My question is, would your killer have tried to shoot me?"

"He has never used a gun before," Frost said. "If he did it, then he's changing his pattern."

"Well, we don't want him to do that," Clint said. "If he does you won't be able to predict his next moves."

"I know," Frost said, "and that disturbs me."

They stood on the corner of Forty-second Street and Broadway and watched the people go by.

"Are there always this many people?" Frost asked, amazed.

"At least," Clint said. "It gets more crowded just before the shows, and just after."

Frost looked around with a lost expression on his face.

"We have a theater district in London, but it's nothing this . . . chaotic. How are we supposed to follow anyone in this?"

"I guess we'll just have to do the best we can," Clint said. "Unless you can come up with a different or better idea?"

"At the moment, no," Frost said.

"Well, then, you can always look on the bright side," Clint said.

"And what would that be, exactly?"

"If you can't see him," Clint said, "then he can't see you."

"Or you," Frost added. "If he *was* the shooter last night, that means he knows who you are, and that you're helping me."

"That's a possibility, all right."

"We might have to rely more on Delvecchio and Eickhorst than we planned."

"Like I said," Clint replied, "they're up to the task. Do you want to stop and get something to drink?"

"Actually, I'd like to get back to the hotel. I find myself very fatigued today."

Clint wondered if that was from spending a night with Brenda. He knew she tired *him* out, and Frost was much younger.

"All right," Clint said. "Let's get a cab."

They rode back to the hotel in silence. Frost seemed lost in thought, and the look on his face was a fearsome frown.

When they reached the hotel and entered the lobby, Clint said, "Inspector Jones came to see me this morning, at breakfast."

"What did he want?"

"You know, I'm not sure," Clint said. "I think he was trying to make up his mind about you."

"Me? Why not you?"

"He spoke to someone about me and got a good report. But he's got no one to speak to about you."

"There is you."

"I don't know you all that well, David," Clint pointed out. "I'm taking into account the fact that James Reed likes you enough to ask me to guide you while you're in this country. But I'm also forming my own opinions about you as we spend time together."

"And what opinions have you formed?"

"You seem to be a good policeman," Clint said, "but you're usually tense, you frown a lot, and you're entirely too obsessed with this killer."

"Obsessed?" Frost seemed to turn the word over in his mind a few times. "Possibly, but I don't think that is a bad thing—not when it comes to a killer."

"You might be right—that might be the only way to catch a killer."

"Indeed," Frost said, "I believe it is. I'll see you later, then. I'm off to my room."

It occurred to Clint, as Frost climbed the stairs, that the man had pleaded fatigue yesterday also, and that had been *before* he met Brenda. He wondered if Frost was ill and not telling him. Could it be that there was something seriously wrong with him, and he was trying to catch this killer while he still could?

Clint hoped that was not the case. Frost was a young man who apparently had a bright future ahead of him. No, maybe he simply had not yet recovered from the long sea voyage.

TWENTY-TWO

To while away the time for the next day or so, Clint wanted
to do some of the things he usually did when he was in
New York: go to museums and shows, eat in good restaurants, and frequent all the different types of bars and saloons that New York had to offer. However, since he only
had the one day to kill, he contented himself with one visit
to one museum, and a very good dinner at Lindy's.

When he returned to the hotel and entered the lobby, he
saw Brenda sitting there.

"Oh, Clint," she said, rushing him, "have you seen David?"

"No," he said, "why?"

"I haven't seen him all day. I thought he'd be in his
room tonight, but he's not."

"I guess he went out."

"But where?" she asked. "He doesn't know where to
go in New York."

"I don't think you need to worry about him, Brenda,"
Clint said. "He's a big boy."

"Oh, I know," she said. "I just . . . well, I have some
news I wanted to share with him."

"What kind of news?"

"I got a part in a show."

"You did? That's wonderful. Congratulations." He gave her a big hug.

"You're so sweet," she said. "I hope you're not mad at me about, uh, David and all. . . ."

"I'm not mad at you, Brenda," Clint told her. "I'm very happy for you. You'll have to tell me what show so I can come and see you."

She told him the name of a show he'd never heard of and then told him where it was playing.

"When do you go on?"

"My first appearance is Monday."

"Well, I'll be right there in the front row to applaud you."

"You *are* sweet," she said, and then sighed. "Well, I guess I'll just go to my room and see if David comes looking for me."

"Brenda, how does he seem to you?" Clint had to ask.

"Well, different," she said. "But he's from a foreign country, after all—and I just love the way he talks."

"I mean, does he seem all right? Healthy, I mean?" Clint persisted.

"Well, he gets tired—but as you know I *can* do that to a man."

"I know that very well," Clint said, "but . . . well, it just seems to me he gets tired too much, even without trying to keep up with you."

"He seems fine to me, Clint."

"Well, okay. Off to your room, then. If I see him I'll tell him you were looking for him."

"All right," she said, "but try not to make me sound so anxious."

"I'll do my best," he said.

He wondered if Frost was tired of Brenda and avoiding her. Maybe he was out on the streets trying to coax the killer into trying for him. Clint hoped he had the Colt Paterson with him—not that he could hit anything with it.

Damn him, but he was taking a chance by leaving the hotel alone.

Clint knew you could go stir-crazy staying inside for too long, but Frost did have Brenda to help while away the hours.

He wondered if he should go looking for the Englishman, but where to look? The only place they had in common was that gun shop on Chambers Street. Could Frost have gone there to practice his shooting alone?

Clint decided not to take that trek to Chambers Street just on the off chance that Frost might be there. Better to sit right here in the lobby and wait until he came back.

TWENTY-THREE

From a doorway directly across the street from the Mayfair Hotel, the killer could see right into the lobby. He watched as Clint had his talk with Brenda. Then, after Brenda left, he watched Clint sit down on one of the lobby sofas.

He had his next victim all picked out, but he wasn't going to kill her until tomorrow. However, if he killed her tonight, it would probably cause enough turmoil to make it worth breaking his pattern.

And since he had set the pattern, he could break it, as well.

He left the doorway and melted into the darkness. . . .

TWENTY-FOUR

Frost came walking into the hotel about an hour later. When he saw Clint, he had the good grace to look chagrined.

"I thought I could get in and out before you got back," he confessed as Clint stood up.

"Are you out there trying to make a target of yourself?"

"I guess . . . maybe I was. I felt bad about you being shot at. If you had been killed last night it would have been my fault."

"I told you, David," Clint said, exasperated, "I get shot at all the time. It's no big deal. If you get yourself killed, though, who's going to catch this killer?"

"You?"

"Not me," Clint said. "I'm just in this to help you. If you get killed I'm not going to be chasing some phantom strangler. I'll let the police handle it."

"We've already seen how they handle things," Frost said.

"Okay, so the New York police are not Scotland Yard; but maybe if we let Jones in on what we're planning to do tomorrow, he might supply some men. We could better our odds of catching the killer before he kills again."

In the beginning it was Clint who hadn't wanted to go

to the police right away. Now it was Frost who was reluctant to go.

"I felt foolish the last time we went," he said. "Let Inspector Jones come to me for help, and I'll help him."

"That's only going to to happen if there's another murder."

"Well," Frost said, "if we have our way, that won't happen. What time are Delvecchio and Eickhorst due tomorrow?"

"Eight A.M. We'll meet here and Delvecchio will tell us what he's worked out."

"Fine," Frost said. "If they're coming that early I'd better get some sleep."

"Uh, Brenda was down here looking for you before," Clint said. "I think she was worried that she couldn't find you."

"She's a sweet girl," Frost said. "Is she in her room?"

"Yes."

"I'll stop in and say good night."

"She may not let you get away with just a good night, you know."

"I know what you mean, but lives will be on the line tomorrow—perhaps even my own. I need to get my sleep. She'll have to understand."

"Well, good luck."

"See you in the morning."

Clint looked around the hotel lobby. He was spending a lot of time either here, in the dining room, or the bar. It would not be smart, however, to go walking around New York at night again.

If what they were planning for tomorrow worked, maybe they'd catch this guy and that would be that. If this went on any further—to a second victim, and a third, and possibly all the way to the sixth—he'd go stir-crazy in this hotel.

• • •

Frost entered Brenda's room and looked down at her on the bed. She was naked, and he could see the bruises around her neck, dark smudges against her fair skin. He knew she was dead. She'd probably been waiting for him when the killer caught her.

He walked around the room, looked out the window, counted to a hundred, then left the room and closed the door behind him.

He went back downstairs to tell Clint Adams that apparently, the killer had decided to change his pattern after all.

TWENTY-FIVE

Inspector Jones would not let Clint or Frost into the room after his arrival, so they were forced to wait downstairs.

"Tell me again," Clint said.

"It's very simple, Clint," Frost replied. "I went to her room, found the door unlocked, and went inside . . . and there she was."

"Dead."

"Naked and dead."

"This son of a bitch you're chasing changed his damn pattern on us," Clint said.

"Yes, he did."

"That doesn't surprise you?"

"To tell the truth," Frost said, "I've been waiting for this."

"You've been *waiting* for it? How come this is the first *I'm* hearing about it?"

"I wasn't sure," Frost told him. "I was just sure enough not to be surprised by it."

"So our whole operation tomorrow is off."

"I would think so," Frost agreed. "It's time to rethink this."

"Oh, I'm going to rethink it, all right," Clint said. "I was in this just to help you, out of friendship for Reed, but now this bastard has me on his trail. I *want* him.''

Just then, Inspector Jones came down to the lobby, where people were milling about because they'd heard that something awful had happened.

Jones looked at two of his uniformed men and said, ''Get these people to their rooms if they have any, out of the hotel if they don't.''

''Yes, sir,'' they both said, and started moving among the crowd. Anyone with a room key was told to go to their room; all others were sent packing.

Jones came over to the sofa where Clint and Frost were sitting.

''Did you both know this girl?''

''Yes,'' they both answered.

Frost added, ''Clint introduced me.''

''And did you both know her . . . well?''

''What are you asking, Inspector?'' Clint wanted to know.

''I think you know what I'm asking, Mr. Adams. Did you both sleep with this girl?''

''I must admit, I did,'' Frost said, ''just last night. Before that . . .''

''Before that she was with me,'' Clint said.

''What do you mean 'with' you?'' Jones asked.

''I think you know what I mean, Inspector.''

''Inspector Frost, I'm going to ask you to go to the other side of the lobby, have a seat, and wait for me. I'd like to talk to the two of you separately.''

''As you wish, Inspector.''

Frost stood up, walked across the room, and sat on another sofa. Jones took the spot vacated by the English detective.

''Let me get this straight,'' he said to Clint. ''She dumped you for him?''

''Essentially, yes, although I wouldn't put it that way. She moved on.''

''And how did that make you feel?''

"Fine. They're closer in age to each other than she and I were."

"You weren't jealous?"

"No."

"Why not?"

"Inspector, I don't have a problem finding willing women."

"So all she was to you was a willing woman?"

"She was a sweet girl who came to New York to be an actress. She didn't deserve to die like that."

"Well," Jones said, "we agree there. What about our Inspector Frost?"

"What about him?"

"He seems a bit of a cold fish after finding the woman he's been sleeping with dead."

"I think that's the way he handles things," Clint said.

"Uh-huh. Well, I'll tell you how I handle things, Mr. Adams. Until I can find out who killed this girl I'd like you and Inspector Frost to stay in town."

"We weren't thinking about leaving."

"What are you thinking about doing?"

"I'm going to catch this bastard."

"And then what are you going to do?"

Clint looked directly into the Inspector's eyes and said, "I think you know what I'm going to do."

Jones stood up and said, "I'm going to pretend I didn't hear that, Adams."

"You can pretend all you want," Clint told him. "It's not going to change my mind."

"And what makes you think you can find him? Frost?" Jones asked.

"No," Clint said, "me. I want this son of a bitch now. He's made a big mistake, because now he's got me after him."

"Leave the police work to the police, Mr. Adams," Jones said. "That's some free advice."

"I'll keep that in mind, Inspector."

"You do that," Jones said, and then walked across the lobby to talk to Frost.

Clint looked across the room to where both inspectors were deep in conversation. *What questions could Jones be asking Frost?* he wondered. *The same ones he'd asked me?* Not likely. After all, Brenda had gone from *his* bed to Frost's, and not the other way around. Clint realized how bad this could make him look in the eyes of the police.

But he really wasn't worried about himself. Brenda was lying upstairs dead, her career and her life cut short much too soon. He'd meant what he said to Inspector Jones. He was going to do whatever it took to find this killer and take care of him.

After Jones finished with Frost, they both walked over to where Clint was sitting. He stood up as they reached him.

"Like I told both of you," Jones said, "I expect you to stay in New York until this is over."

"I am not going anywhere, Inspector," Frost said. "I am going to do what I came here to do."

"That goes for me, too," Clint said.

"Fine," Jones said, "but I'm warning both of you: Don't get in my way."

"Can we go up—" Clint started, but Jones cut him off.

"No, I still have some people coming in, and we've got to remove the body. Why don't you two go get yourselves a drink. We should be done in about an hour."

Clint looked at Frost, who shrugged and said, "Why not?"

TWENTY-SIX

They tried to come up with a new strategy, and an explanation, over a drink.

"Why Brenda?" Clint asked out loud. He'd been thinking it for hours.

"Well, she was an actress."

Clint passed a hand over his face.

"She just got a part in a show, too. She was going to start Monday."

"I know," Frost said. "It's a damn shame."

"It's more than that," Clint said. "It's . . . it's . . . I can't think of a word vile enough." He looked at Frost. "Why did he pick her? Was it at random, or did he know about you and her?"

"It could be a coincidence."

"I hate coincidences. There'd have to be too damn many. Can it be a coincidence that he picked a woman who was staying in the same hotel as we are? Who we had both been with? No, Frost, this nut is watching us very carefully."

He looked around the room, which was empty except for some policemen.

"He could have been anyone in this lobby tonight, watching us, laughing at us."

"Somebody must have seen something," Frost said.

"We should go door to door on that floor and ask questions."

"The police should be doing that."

"They won't," Frost said, "not until morning. We should do it now, wake people up and ask them questions. They're less bound to lie then."

"You might be right about that."

"Meanwhile, I've got to get inside his head and figure out what he's thinking."

"Why did he change his pattern?" Clint asked. "Why now?"

"Because he can," Frost said. "That way he's in complete control of the situation."

"So there's no telling what he'll do next?"

"What he'll do next is look for his next victim."

"Man or woman?" Clint wanted to know.

"According to his London pattern another woman, but now, who knows?"

"Make an educated guess," Clint said, "based on your history with him. If he's trying to play with our heads, what's he going to do?"

"Well," Frost said, "he'll think that we think he's off his pattern and that he'll go after a man, now."

"But you think he'll still go after a woman?"

"Yes."

"Why?"

"Because," Frost said, "he doesn't want us to think there's a pattern at all—but he's a creature of habit. He may not keep the *same* pattern, but there will still be a pattern."

"And all we have to do is figure out what it is."

"Right. We can still use your two friends when they arrive tomorrow morning."

"I forgot about them," Clint said. "They'll be here in about seven hours."

"We need to get some sleep, then."

"What about waking people up and questioning them?"

"We can do it with the rooms closest to her—across the hall, on either side. Somebody may have heard something useful."

"Let's do it, then," Clint said. "The police should be just about finished."

They stood up and walked back to the lobby. Two policemen were walking to the front door carrying a stretcher with Brenda Benet's body on it, covered by a sheet.

"I guess they're done," Clint said.

TWENTY-SEVEN

Clint and Frost questioned the people on either side of Brenda's room and across the hall, letting them think that they were policemen. One of them, a middle–aged woman in the room on the right of Brenda's, said she thought she heard some commotion in the room, but just thought it was Brenda and a gentleman caller.

"Any particular gentleman caller?" Clint asked the woman.

"Well," she replied, "I thought it was probably one of you."

She didn't remember the time, only that she had already turned in.

"And what time was that?" Frost asked.

"I went to bed at eight."

They thanked her and moved on. The other people had heard nothing, and didn't appreciate being awakened, police or not.

"Well," Clint said, after they'd talked to the last person, "I guess we better turn in. We can discuss over breakfast what our next move is going to be."

"Clint," Frost said, touching his arm. "I just want to say . . . it may not seem that I'm distraught over Brenda's death, but . . . I've trained myself to keep my emotions in check.''

"That's all right, David. I said the very same thing to Inspector Jones when he asked me about your reaction.''

"He asked you about me?''

"Yes.''

"Well, he asked me about you, too,'' Frost said.

"Oh? What did he ask?''

"He asked if I thought you were jealous of Brenda and me.''

"And what did you tell him?''

"I told him that was ridiculous, that you and I had discussed it and there was no problem.''

"Well, good,'' Clint said. "Now maybe he'll stop questioning us and start looking for the real killer.''

Frost's room was right there on the third floor, but Clint had to walk down to the second. He sat on the bed and heaved a sigh. He was dead tired, but it didn't seem right to sleep after what had happened to Brenda.

That was his last conscious thought until the sun streaming through the window woke him up.

TWENTY-EIGHT

He awoke lying on the bed, fully dressed, gun and all. He removed the gun from his belt, and then took off his shirt and washed up in the basin on the dresser. He dried himself off and put on a clean shirt. He went down to see if Delvecchio and Eickhorst had arrived yet. When he got to the lobby they were both there.

"What the hell happened last night?" Delvecchio asked. "This place is buzzing."

"Come with me to breakfast and I'll tell you."

They went into the dining room, ordered coffee and breakfast, and then Clint related the events of the previous evening.

"You mean this killer changed his pattern, after all?" Eickhorst asked.

"That's right."

"What about him picking a girl you both knew?" Delvecchio asked. "Coincidence?"

"I don't think so."

"I didn't think you would." Delvecchio knew him at least *that* well.

"I'm sorry about the girl, Clint," Eickhorst said.

"Well, the killer is going to be sorrier," Clint said, "because now I'm after him for personal reasons."

"Speaking of personal reasons," Delvecchio said, "where's our good inspector?"

"We got to bed late last night," Clint said. "Maybe he overslept. He'll be along."

The waiter came with their breakfast, passed out the plates, and retreated back to the kitchen.

"So what happens to our little excursion today to Broadway?" Delvecchio asked.

"It's off," Clint said. "We'll have to try and figure out his new pattern."

"What if there is no new pattern?"

"Frost thinks there will be," Clint said. "He thinks the killer needs a pattern—and since he just broke the old one, he'll have to come up with a new one."

"I don't know how he's going to do that," Delvecchio said.

"Frost seems pretty odd, don't you fellas think?" Eickhorst asked.

"Well, yeah," Delvecchio said, "although I didn't want to bring it up."

"Well, he's obsessed with catching this killer, I know that," Clint said.

"Maybe the obsession is making him a little crazy," Delvecchio said.

"If that's the case," Eickhorst said, "finding the body of the girl is not going to help."

At that moment, Clint saw Frost enter the dining room. "Here he comes," he warned the others.

All three men stood and shook hands with Frost, and then the four of them sat. The waiter hurried over; Frost told him just to bring him what everyone else was having.

"We heard about what happened last night," Delvecchio said. "How are you holding up?"

"Fine," Frost said. "I mean, it was something of a shock, but I have seen dead bodies before."

Delvecchio and Eickhorst exchanged a look and Clint

knew they were thinking the same thing Inspector Jones had said the night before: "goldfish."

"So this changes things," Delvecchio said to Frost.

"Yes, it does," Frost said, "but if you gentlemen still want to help . . ."

"We're here to help," Delvecchio said.

"What would you like us to do?" Eickhorst added.

"Ask questions around the hotel," Frost said, "inside, outside, guests, staff; someone must have seen something that we can use."

"All right," Delvecchio said. "That's what we'll spend today doing, then."

"What will you and I be doing?" Clint asked Frost.

"Something that should have occurred to me before," the Englishman said.

"And what's that?"

He didn't answer, preferring to wait until the waiter had distributed their plates.

"The docks," he said finally, as the man moved away. "We should go down to the docks and check with some of the ships. If we can find the one the killer came in on, maybe we can find where he's staying."

"That's as good an idea as any," Clint said. "There were probably a bunch of passengers from England, but we do have a pretty general description."

"He would have been a loner on the ship, and perhaps for that reason might have stood out."

"Why do you say that?" Delvecchio asked.

"He would not have wanted to kill anyone on the ship," Frost explained. "It was too isolated, and he'd be taking too much of a chance. If he was around people I believe he would have lost control."

"Okay," Clint said, "so we're looking for an average-looking loner."

"I have a question," Eickhorst said.

"What?" Frost asked.

"How are the New York police going to feel about us conducting an unauthorized investigation?"

"Well, I cannot lie to you," Frost said. "They are not going to like it at all."

Delvecchio looked around the table, then smiled and said, "That works for me."

TWENTY-NINE

Clint and Frost left Delvecchio and Eickhorst at the hotel to conduct their "investigation" and went down to the New York harbor. They had to check in with the harbormaster to find out what ships had docked recently from Europe. Frost figured, just to play it safe, they should go back two weeks.

"We go back that far," the harbormaster said, "but some of them ships have gone back out again."

"All right, then, a week," Frost said, adding to Clint, "He can't have had that much more of a head start on me."

"You fellas mind tellin' me what you want this information for?" the man asked.

"How about for ten dollars?" Clint said.

Armed with a list of five boats that had docked in the past week, they went down to the docks to find them. In each case it took a while to find the captain, and when they did find them—to a man—they claimed not to know who was on their ship.

"We're not a luxury liner," one captain said. "If someone books passage on my ship they have to work."

Clint and Frost exchanged a glance. If the killer worked

for his passage, then maybe one of the crew would remember him.

"What about your crew?" Clint asked. "Would they remember him?"

"Maybe."

"Can we talk to them?"

"You can talk to the ones who are onboard," he said, "but that's just a skeleton crew."

"Where are the others?" Frost asked.

"Gone."

"Gone where?" Clint asked.

"To the four corners of the earth, for all I know," the man said, with a shrug.

"If that's the case, Captain, how will you ship out?" Clint asked.

"You don't know much about ships, do you, lad?"

"No, I don't," Clint said.

"The crew that's onboard are my permanent crew. All the others sign up for one trip, or for a month, or however long they have to to forget the girl who threw them over. Understand?"

"We understand," Frost said. "May we question the members of the crew who are onboard?"

"Go ahead, though I don't know what good it will do you."

"What about your first mate?" Clint asked. "Wouldn't he be the one who signs up the new men?"

"He was, and he would be, but he's dead."

Both Clint and Frost stopped for a moment, and then the Englishman said, "What?"

"Dead," the captain repeated. "He didn't make the whole trip."

"How did he die?"

"Damndest thing," the captain said. "One of the ropes from the mainsail somehow got caught around his neck, and it hung him."

Frost looked at Clint and knew they were thinking the

same thing. A rope around the neck would effectively hide the finger marks left by manual strangulation.

"Well," Clint said, "in any case we'd like to talk to your permanent crew."

"Have at it, then," the captain said. "Just watch your step. I don't want to find either of you hung up by the mainsail."

"We'll do our best to make sure that doesn't happen, Captain," Clint said.

THIRTY

Clint and Frost spent the remainder of the day questioning the crew members who were still onboard. Their task seemed hopeless, however, judging by the reaction of the first crew member they questioned.

"Jesus, mate," he said to Clint, "you described half the men onboard. Don't you have a better description than that?"

"I'm afraid not," Clint said. "You see, nobody's ever seen him."

"What's he done, anyway?" another man asked.

"He kills people," Clint said.

"Strangles them," Frost added. "Men and women."

"He's a fiend, then?" another crew member asked. Frost had told Clint that this man was from his country and had a cockney accent.

"That he is," Frost said, "the biggest fiend there ever was."

"Well, we wish we could help you, mates, we really do," the first crew member said, "but you ain't given us much to go on."

"He would have kept to himself," Frost said. "Probably would have come out at night."

The three men exchanged blank glances and then shook their heads.

"That don't ring no bells," one of them said.

"Well, thanks, anyway," Clint said. "Maybe we're just on the wrong boat."

They left that boat and Frost said, "Well, we might as well go back to the hotel. Maybe Delvecchio or Eickhorst have found something out."

"There's still one ship to check," Clint said, pointing.

"We don't have to check that one, Clint," Frost said.

"Why not?"

"Because," Frost said, "that's the one *I* came in on."

The killer watched Clint very carefully. Unbeknownst to Clint, the killer was very close, close enough to see his eyes. How did it feel, he wondered, to have spent a day in total futility? They had found out exactly nothing that could help them. He had killed two people since arriving in New York, and they were still without a clue.

The great Clint Adams, the Gunsmith. This was a contest the killer was really starting to enjoy.

THIRTY-ONE

When they got back to the hotel, Clint said, "I'm tired of this place."

"So am I," Frost agreed.

"It reminds me of Brenda—not that I could ever forget—but I just don't like it here."

"We should move to another hotel," Frost said. "That might help."

"That's a good idea," Clint said. "I'm going to collect my gear and do that."

"I wouldn't know where to go, so I will . . . tag along?"

"Yes," Clint said, "tag along is right, but first we need to find Del and Anson. We can't leave until they come back."

"But we can still pack and check out."

"Okay. I'll see you back here in half an hour?"

"Make it twenty minutes," Frost said. "I packed very light."

"Twenty minutes, it is."

Twenty-five minutes later they had checked out of the hotel and were waiting in the lobby for the other two men to arrive. Before they did, however, Inspector Jones came walking through the front door.

"Looks like you gents plan on traveling," he said.

"Do you have someone watching us?" Clint asked.

"Yes," Jones said, "and he told me that you were packed and checked out."

"That's right," Clint said, "we are."

"And headed where?"

"Another hotel."

"Here in Manhattan?"

"Of course, here in Manhattan."

"Ah," Jones said, nodding as if he understood, "too many bad memories here."

Neither Clint nor Frost replied to that.

"So you've made a trip down here for nothing, Inspector," Clint said. "We're not leaving town."

"That's good, that's very good," Jones said, "but there's another problem I have that maybe you can help me with."

"And what would that be?"

"I've got two men locked up in a jail cell who say they're friends of yours."

"What?" Clint exclaimed.

"One's name is Delvecchio, and he's a detective," Jones said. "The other one's name is . . . whatever . . . and I don't know *what* he is, except they say they're friends of yours. Is this true?"

"Yes, it is," Clint said.

"What did you arrest them for?" Frost asked.

"I'm not sure yet," Jones said. "They were walking around here, asking all kinds of questions about the murder. Why do you suppose they were doing that?"

"Maybe because we asked them to," Clint said.

"Ah," Jones said, "now we get to it. When I told you boys to stay out of this investigation that meant your friends, too."

"How do we get them out?"

Jones studied them both for a few moments, then shook his head.

"I'll release them to you," he said, finally, "but you've got to keep them out of my hair."

"Fine," Clint said, "they're out."

"And you two have to stay out of my hair, as well," Jones added, pointing at them for emphasis.

"Agreed," Frost said, "we're out."

"Why don't I believe you?" he asked.

"Believe me, Inspector," Clint said, "we're all going to do our best to keep out of your hair."

Jones studied them some more. "I'm going back to Mulberry Street to let them out. Just remember what I said."

"We'll remember," Clint said, "and thanks for letting them go."

Jones looked like he wanted to make some more threats, but he finally just turned and walked away.

"Now what do we do?" Frost asked.

"Well, we'll wait for Del and Anson to show up, and then we'll go and find another hotel."

"Do you have one in mind?"

"Actually," Clint said, "I do. It's more of a rooming house than a hotel, though—although not quite a rooming house. I mean, they give you a room, but they don't feed you."

"We can get our own food," Frost said. "It sounds like the kind of place the killer wouldn't expect us to go."

"My thoughts exactly."

They sat on one of the sofas to await the arrival of their two colleagues.

"I guess checking out the boats was a bust," Clint said.

"It was just an idea that didn't pan out," Frost said. "That happens a lot in an investigation."

"I know . . . it's frustrating, sometimes."

"Try 'often.' "

"Why do you do it, then?"

Frost shrugged. "I love being a policeman."

"And yet you're risking your job to track this killer."

"I guess I hate him," Frost said, "more than I like my job."

Clint couldn't argue that because, right now, he hated the killer, too.

THIRTY-TWO

When Delvecchio and Eickhorst arrived, Clint told them that he and Frost were changing locations to Decatur House. Clint had never been to the rooming house, but he'd been told about it. It was on Forty-third Street between Tenth and Eleventh Avenues.

"The killer knows we're here," he explained.

"How are you going to get to the other place without him knowing?" Delvecchio asked.

"That's your job," Clint said. "Get us two cabs and give the drivers directions that nobody else could follow. Got it?"

"I got it," Delvecchio said.

While they waited for him to get back, Eickhorst said, "You got us out of jail." It wasn't a question.

"That's right."

"How?"

"I promised we'd all stay out of Inspector Jones's hair."

"And how are we supposed to do that?"

"By not getting caught anymore," Clint said. "We'll just have to real careful and discreet."

"Discretion is not my long suit," Eickhorst said, "but I'll try."

Delvecchio returned.

"Okay, I found a cabdriver who's willing to take a long route to where we're going. He's, uh, gonna charge us double the fare."

"That's fine," Frost said. "I can take care of it."

"We'll split it," Clint said. "Del, you and I will go in one cab, Anson, you and Inspector Frost are in the other."

"But we're all gonna end up in the same place, right?" Eickhorst asked.

"Right," Clint said. "If the killer wants to follow, he's going to have to pick one of us. And since he's from England, if our cabdrivers take some shortcuts they'll be able to lose him."

"Then we'll have a sanctuary," Delvecchio said.

"That's the point," Clint said. "Let's go."

They piled into the two cabs and pulled away from the Mayfair Hotel. Clint felt a rush of sadness again over the death of Brenda Benet, but then it gave way to the determination to see her killer brought to justice—his justice.

"How's our friend doin'?" Delvecchio asked.

"He's okay."

"Hasn't broken down into tears yet?"

"And he won't. He feels badly about Brenda, but he won't let that interfere with what he's doing."

"Clint, I have an idea."

"Let's hear it."

"I think Anson and I should also stay at Decatur House."

"Have you been there before?" Clint asked.

"No, but I've heard of it. They usually have some rooms available. Anson and I could even share one. That way we'd all be in the same place."

"Sounds good to me."

"Do you, uh, think Frost will pay for it?"

"He and I are going to be splitting expenses from now on."

"Why? I thought this killer was his."

"That's where you—and he—are wrong, because as of yesterday this killer is mine."

THIRTY-THREE

When they reached Decatur House they were able to get three rooms: one each for Clint and Frost, and one for both Delvecchio and Eickhorst.

The Decatur was in a very old building that someone had spent a lot of money renovating inside. Clint was also willing to bet that the building wasn't quite as rickety as it looked.

When they entered they were met by a small man with a good handshake, who asked if he could help them.

"We need some rooms," Clint said, and they negotiated the price for three.

"Now, you understand we have no food here?" the man asked. "We do have maids who will clean your rooms, though, if you like."

"Not for me," Frost said.

"Me, neither," Clint said.

"We're not that dirty," Delvecchio said, and Eickhorst nodded.

"That's fine, then," the man said. "My name is Mr. Reynolds, and I welcome you all to Decatur House."

Clint got settled in his room, which, as it turned out, was larger than the other two rooms. They were all just down

117

a hall from each other so he knocked on the other two doors, told them how large his room was and that they'd meet there in ten minutes.

Frost was the first to arrive. He crossed the floor and peered out the window, which overlooked Forty-third Street.

"My room overlooks a back alley," Frost said, "and the sides of the building are sheer, as are yours."

"That's good," Clint said. "See anything out there?"

"No," Frost said, "nothing. I don't think he knows where we are now."

There was a knock and then Delvecchio and Eickhorst entered.

"Jeez," Delvecchio said, "this is twice the size of our room, and we're sharing."

"One bed," Clint said.

"I see that. We got two, but there ain't much to the mattresses."

"We have to go out," Eickhorst said abruptly.

"Where?" Frost asked.

"If we're gonna be stayin' here we'll need some clothes, and supplies."

Clint put his hand in his pocket and came out with some money.

"Here—"

Eickhorst cut him off with a chopping motion of his hand. "Why don't we settle up when this is all over, okay?"

"Sure," Clint said.

"Thank you both for your help," Frost said.

"I know a place we can get outfitted, and it ain't anywhere this killer is gonna see us. We'll be back in about an hour."

"Okay," Clint said. "While you're at it, see if you can't think of a place to eat that the killer won't find."

"I know just the place," Delvecchio said. "See ya in a little while."

Delvecchio and Eickhorst left, and Clint looked at Frost.

"Okay, Inspector," he said, "you're the one with the predictions. What's your man going to do next?"

"He'll have to kill again, and soon," Frost said. "I just need to figure out where, and who?"

"Is that all?" Clint asked. "Hell, you'll have that figured out before those two get back from their shopping spree."

"Is that an American trait?" Frost asked.

"What?"

"Sarcasm."

"Oh, yeah."

THIRTY-FOUR

Clint didn't like waiting around for Frost to get an idea, so he started trying to put himself in the killer's head.

Let's say the killer knows that Frost is here, looking for him, he thought. *He knows that I'm helping him; he's already killed twice, and broke his established pattern while doing it.*

What's his next pattern going to be?

And does he know who Clint Adams is?

If Frost had these strong feelings about the killer, what if they were reciprocated? The killer was going to want to make a fool out of Scotland Yard Inspector David Frost.

How would he do that?

Clint left his room, walked down to Frost's, and knocked on the door. When the man answered he was groggy, obviously fresh from a nap.

"Clint. Are they back yet?"

"No," Clint said. "I've been doing some thinking, David, and I'd like to come in and brainstorm a bit with you."

"Come right in," Frost said. "I could use a brainstorm, right now."

Clint entered and Frost closed the door behind him.

"What's on your mind?"

"I think the killer is going to strike tonight," Clint said.

"So soon after the first one? What makes you think that?"

"I'm trying to do what you do, put myself into his mind."

"And?"

"And I think he wants to make a fool of you—of all of us, you, me, and the New York City police. I don't think he's going to wait. If he always kills a total of six people, then I think he's going to kill for the next four days."

Frost sat on the bed and looked up at Clint.

"That's a frightening thought."

"I know it is. We have to stop him."

"Obviously," Frost said. "But how?"

"We're going to have to figure out who his next victim is. First, will it be a man or a woman?"

Frost thought a moment, then said, "A woman."

"Why?"

"Because four of the six he killed in London were women, and because that sends a message to us that we can't stop him. I believe he *knew* how upset we'd be after Brenda was killed. I think he's going to go after another woman."

"Another actress?"

"Maybe."

"So maybe we should go ahead with what we had planned for Times Square," Clint suggested.

"We can do that," Frost said. "We need Mr. Delvecchio to tell us what he had set up."

"They should be back soon," Clint said. "We can get over there before dark and get situated."

"This is still a long shot," Frost said, running his hand through his hair. For the first time Clint realized that the man look disheveled. He wasn't used to seeing the usually cool, calm, and confident Englishman in this state.

"Are you all right, David?"

"Hmm? Oh, I'm fine. I just . . . I hadn't anticipated it being this hard."

"You thought it would be easy?"

Frost hesitated before answering.

"Not easy," he said, finally, "but I thought I'd be able to figure him out."

"Well," Clint said, "as they say in baseball, he threw you a curve."

"He . . . threw me a what?" Frost asked, looking puzzled.

"Never mind . . ." Clint said.

THIRTY-FIVE

When Delvecchio and Eickhorst returned, freshly outfitted, Clint and Frost told them what they'd decided to do.

"Del," Clint said, afterward, "we'll need your plan for Broadway."

"I've got it right here," Delvecchio said, tapping his head. "All we have to do is go down there and I'll situate you all."

"Okay, then," Clint said. "Is everybody armed?"

Delvecchio and Eickhorst both nodded. Wherever their guns were, they were well hidden.

"David?"

"I have both guns," Frost said. "Should I bring the Navy Colt?"

"Only if you want to shoot through a building," Delvecchio said.

"Bring the Colt Paterson, David," Clint said. "You'll want to get close anyway, won't you?"

"Oh, yes," Frost said. "Very close."

"Okay, then," Clint said. "You get your gun and we'll be on our way."

Frost nodded and left them to go to his room.

"Clint," Delvecchio asked, "what happens when we find this killer?"

125

"I think Frost and I are going to argue over who kills him."

"Aren't you gonna turn him in to the police?" Eickhorst asked.

Clint studied the man's face and decided to give him the answer he was waiting for.

"Sure, Anson," he said, "sure we are."

Eickhorst's look turned dubious, but he didn't pursue the matter. At least now both he and Delvecchio could claim they knew nothing about any plan to kill the killer.

Broadway was New York's glittering Great White Way from Forty-second Street down to Madison Square, which covered roughly ten blocks or so. So the four men had to find some way to cover ten blocks.

Delvecchio had studied the situation and had picked out four spots along the ten-block area. He left Eickhorst at the first one, closest to Forty-second Street. Then they walked a few blocks and Clint took up his position. The next one—the one closest to the theater district—would be for Frost, and Delvecchio would go down around Madison Square.

"Do we really need to cover the full extent of this section?" Frost asked, after they had left Clint at his position.

"We don't know where this nut is going to be, Frost," Delvecchio said. "We're better off covering too much ground than not enough, don't you think?"

"Actually, I think you're right."

Delvecchio left Frost at his position and walked the rest of the way to Madison Square. Along the way he saw any number of fashionably dressed, beautiful women and wondered, How were they supposed to pick out the killer's potential victim from all these?

Then again, the girl he chose probably would not be so fashionably dressed. She'd be an actress, and maybe one who didn't have the money to dress real well, but who she'd be beautiful.

Those might be a little easier to spot, but not by much.

•   •   •

At his position along Broadway, around Thirty-eighth Street, Clint was having much the same thoughts. There was no shortage of women along this stretch, as there were almost as many shops catering to them as there were saloons for the men.

This plan did not seem as sound as it had the first time they thought of it, but it was the only plan they had.

THIRTY-SIX

They spent the day in their positions on Broadway. The longer it went the sillier the whole idea seemed to Clint. He decided to go into a saloon across the street and sit by the window while he had a beer. It was against his nature to sit in the window of any establishment, making a target of himself, but this was a special case.

Over a beer he wondered what they had thought they could accomplish this way. Was he supposed to spot a likely looking young actress and follow her? All four of them could each end up following a girl, and it could still be the wrong girl. Meanwhile, the killer would be stalking the right girl—if his next victim was a girl, at all.

He nursed the beer until it was almost warm. By then it was close to four o'clock and they'd been there for the better part of six hours. He decided to walk down to where Frost was and discuss the situation with him.

The killer spotted her around three o'clock. She was perfect. Beautiful, with clear, white skin and a ripe figure in a dress that had seen better days. A struggling actress, to be sure, on the way home from rehearsals.

He followed her, which was at the same time easy to do, but difficult. Easy because he was able to hide among all the other people, but difficult because they got in his way. She left Broadway and walked west, until she reached Ninth Avenue, where the glitz of the Great White Way was gone. On Thirty-first Street, between Ninth and Tenth Avenues, she stopped and entered a building, where she probably had a room. He waited a little while to see if she would come back out, even went to the door to check and see if it might be someplace she was just visiting, like a doctor's office. As he watched, other people came and went, and he became convinced that this was where she lived. He also made sure he knew exactly where the building was situated, so he could return to it at night.

Later *that* night.

When Clint got down to around Thirty-fifth Street he didn't see Frost anywhere. He figured maybe the man had ducked into a saloon as he had done and started looking in windows, but he didn't see him.

Of course, the other alternative was that he'd seen a girl he thought would be a likely victim and was following her.

He wondered about going back to his own position, but the whole thing just seemed futile to him. He was about to continue walking, heading for Delvecchio's position, when he saw Frost come from around the corner. The man's stride faltered just for a moment when he saw Clint.

"Where've you been?" Clint asked. "I thought maybe you were following some girl."

"I had a call," Frost said, hitching up his pants. "What are you doing here?"

"I got to thinking how futile this really is," Clint said. "There are so many women . . ."

"I know," Frost said. "I have been feeling the same way."

"Think we ought to call it off?"

Frost looked at his watch and said, "Why not?"

"Okay," Clint said. "I'll walk back up Broadway and

tell Anson, you walk down and tell Delvecchio. We'll meet back at the Decatur.''

"All right," Frost said, and then he added, "He's going to hit again tonight, you know."

Clint nodded and said, "That's what I'm afraid of."

THIRTY-SEVEN

Clint and Eickhorst got back to the Decatur well before Frost and Delvecchio.

"Wonder what's keeping them," Eickhorst said as they stood out in front of the building, waiting for their two colleagues to arrive.

"Maybe they ran into something."

"Like what? The murderer? In the act?"

"That'd be too much to ask for, wouldn't it?" Clint asked.

"I'm afraid so. You know, I had the same thoughts you had all along about this 'plan,' but I didn't want to say anything."

"I know," Clint said. "Seems like a wasted day now, doesn't it?"

"Yeah, it does. Wait, there they are. They just turned the corner."

Clint looked down the block and saw that Eickhorst was right. Apparently they'd all walked back to the Decatur; since Clint had walked from Eickhorst's position, they had been closer.

When the two men reached them the four of them simply remained outside, on the front steps of the building. For a few moments nobody said anything.

"Well," Delvecchio finally said, "what's next?"

Clint and Frost exchanged a glance. The Scotland Yard man looked worn out.

"We haven't figured that out yet," Clint said. "I guess you guys are on your own for the rest of the evening."

"Sounds good to me," Delvecchio said. "I met a couple of women over on Broadway who invited me out—if I could find a friend." He looked at Eickhorst.

"Who are you kidding?" the other man asked. "I'm probably the only friend you've got."

"Well, let's go up and change into something pretty, then," Delvecchio said. "We'll see you fellas later."

Delvecchio and Eickhorst went inside, and Clint and Frost sat down on the steps.

"What *do* we do now?" Clint asked.

"He's out there," Frost said. He buried the heels of his hands in his eye sockets for a moment. "I can still feel him."

"Which means he's probably going to hit again tonight, and there's nothing we can do to stop him."

"Hopefully," Frost said, "he'll leave some kind of clue this time."

"Has he ever left a clue before?"

"Not one that panned out."

"Then why hope for one now?"

"Because we need it," Frost said. "We need *something*."

THIRTY-EIGHT

The killer approached the building, keeping to the shadows as he went. He wore dark clothing, and a black cape with black velvet lining. He loved wearing that cape, even wore it sometimes when he *wasn't* looking for a victim.

He stopped before he reached the building he'd followed the girl to earlier in the day. He knew when he killed her his pursuers were really going to feel it—and this was only number three. Wait until he got to number six.

And would he stop there?

He didn't know, at the moment. He was too busy imagining what was going to happen with number three.

He went around to the back of the house where, he knew, he'd find a flimsy door. These doors were like his best friends.

He forced the door without much sound and entered the house. He knew there were other lodgers who might wake up at any minute, but that just made it more exciting.

He found the stairs and started up. What was most exciting was that he didn't know what room the girl was in. He was going to have to open the door to every room and look in on the occupant without waking them, until he found the room he was looking for.

Somebody might wake up, but if they did—well, there'd be two victims tonight, wouldn't there?

THIRTY-NINE

Inspector Jones looked down at the dead girl. Her head was at an odd angle, meaning she'd not only been strangled, but her neck had been broken.

"Inspector?"

He turned and saw Officer Murphy coming toward him. Murphy was the first policeman on the scene. The body had been discovered by the woman who ran the house, and she had immediately sent for the police.

They had sent a runner to Jones's house to rouse him, but they didn't wake him, they simply made him get up off his naked wife much sooner than he'd intended. That was a lost opportunity. Martha Jones didn't get in the mood very often anymore. He'd probably have to wait weeks now . . .

"What is it, Murphy?"

"We got another one."

"What?"

"Down the hall. I was canvassing, like you said, questioning the other tenants. I knocked on the door of this one room and nobody opened the door. The owner saw me and told me that the occupant—a Mr. Ralph Norris—should still be inside. She opened the door for me with her key and, well . . . there he was."

Jones heaved a sigh, waved and said, "Take me there, Murphy."

"Yes, sir."

When Clint came down from his room the next morning, none of his colleagues were around. Well, there was no hard-and-fast rule that they had to eat together, was there? He decided that instead of knocking on their doors, he'd just go out and find someplace to have breakfast.

He went out the front door and looked around before descending the steps. This killer was a resourceful son of a bitch, and there was no telling whether or not he'd managed to locate them. Maybe he had followed them back from Broadway last night.

He stopped at the bottom of the steps and waited. When there were no shots, he turned left and walked up the block, to Ninth Avenue.

All along Ninth Avenue he saw shops, and a few restaurants. New York was a wonderful place to eat, he thought, so many different cafés and saloons and restaurants.

He walked a few blocks and then picked a place that looked nice. It didn't look like the owners spent too much money on ambience, so maybe the food would be good.

He went inside.

Jones stared down at the dead man, who was also naked. He was a big man, well built, but seemingly shrunken in death.

Jones bent down to examine the body.

"Strangled," he said, "like the girl."

"Yes, sir."

Jones looked up at Murphy.

"Nobody heard anything from this room, either?" he asked.

"I don't know, sir," Murphy said. "I only asked about the other one."

"Well, go and ask about this one, Officer."

"Yes, sir."

"Damn," Jones said, standing up. Two dead bodies in the same building. Why? Was one a victim and the other . . . what? A mistake? Had the killer entered the wrong room, making it necessary to kill the occupant?

He turned to look at the door, where a uniformed policeman stood.

"Watch over this body until we can have it removed."

"Yes, sir."

"Nobody gets in, got it?"

"Yes, sir, I've got it."

Jones went back down the hall to the woman's room. The owner, Ralph Reynolds was out in the hall.

"Did she have any boyfriends?" Jones asked him.

"I don't know," he said. "Not here, I know that. We don't allow that here."

Jones thought about both bodies being naked. Did they sleep that way, or had the killer stripped them after he finished with them? Or maybe the man was nude because he hadn't been alone. If that were the case, where was his girlfriend? Had the killer graduated to kidnapping?

"What's her name?" he asked Reynolds.

The man rubbed his graying stubble and said, "Linda, or Lenore . . . something like that . . . what was it . . . Leann, that's it."

"Leann?" the policeman repeated.

"Yes, sir."

"What's her last name?"

"I don't know."

"Don't your guests check in?"

"No," Reynolds said, "as long as they pay for their room, their names are their own business."

"I see," Jones said. "You wouldn't have any jailbirds living in this house, would you, Mr. Reynolds?"

If the dead man was a criminal, that might explain his death.

"I only rent to nice people," Reynolds said indignantly.

"Whose names you don't ask for."

"Money talks," he said. "That's all I care about."

"Was this little gal paid up?"

"Well . . ."

"I guess not."

"She's an actress, and she ain't—didn't—have much money."

"So," Jones said, "out of the goodness of your heart you let her stay here."

"That's right," the man agreed, "the goodness of my heart."

"Reynolds," Jones said, "you don't expect me to swallow that, do you?"

"Whataya mean?"

"I mean, what were you getting from her besides money?" Jones asked.

"Hey, I don't—"

The inspector put one hand flat against the man's chest and pinned him to the wall. Norris was in his fifties, and was not a big man.

"Okay, okay," he said, "so I visited her room once in a while. You seen her, she's really pretty, got really nice little tits—"

"Never mind that," Jones said. "Were you with her tonight?"

"Well . . . yeah, earlier . . ."

That explained why she was naked.

"Good thing you weren't with her when the killer came knocking," Jones said, releasing the man. "You'd be dead now."

"Jesus!" Reynolds said, his eyes bugging out as he realized what Jones said was true.

Two policemen appeared at the end of the hall with a stretcher, and Jones said to the man, "Make way."

Reynolds moved out of the way, asking, "Do you still need me?"

"If I need you I'll find you," Jones said. "You can go."

"You know," he continued, "I never forced her—"

"Just shut up and go," Jones said. He turned away from Reynolds and shouted, "Murphy!"

"Here, Inspector," Murphy said, coming down the hall. "One tenant said he thought he heard something from one of the rooms, but he just thought that the girl—Miss Leann Frasier—was paying her rent. See, when she didn't have the money, the landlord, Reynolds, would—"

"I know what the landlord did, Murphy," Jones said. "I've got another job for you, and to get it done I want you to get all the help you need."

"What's the job, sir?"

"Find me Clint Adams."

"How do I do that, sir?"

"You look, damn it!" Jones snapped. "Get some men and go out and look for him."

"But he left his hotel—"

"I know he left his hotel," Jones said. "I got that from the man who was supposed to be watching him. By the way, *he* works out in Brooklyn now. Get my meaning?"

"Yes, sir!"

"Start up around Ninth and Tenth Avenues, some of the flophouses. My guess is they moved so they could stay someplace and keep low."

"Yes, sir," Murphy said, "I'll take care of it."

Clint was eating his breakfast when the two uniformed policeman enter the café. The food had been good, the coffee better, but there was something about the way these policemen were looking at him. They remained in the doorway for a few moments, and then a man in a worn, brown hat entered. He spoke with the uniforms and then approached Clint's table.

"Mr. Adams?"

"That's right."

"I'm Officer John Murphy, sir," the man said. "Inspector Jones would like to see you."

"What about?"

"There's been more murders, sir."

"Jesus," Clint said, shaking his head. "Wait. You said *more murders?*"

"Yes, sir," Murphy said. "More than one."

"Where?"

"I can take you there, sir. I believe the inspector will still be there."

"All right, let's go."

He stood up.

"Just out of curiosity, Officer," Clint said. "How did you find me?"

"I looked . . . sir."

FORTY

They brought Clint right to the first room, where the girl was lying dead.

"Damn it," he said, looking down at the pathetic remains of what was once a lovely girl.

"Another one down the hall," Jones said. "A man, also naked."

"Did he—"

"Undress them?" Jones finished. "Well, not her. Apparently the landlord takes her rent out in trade, the old lech."

Clint winced.

"Was she an actress?"

"That's what we've been told."

Was it worth it? he wondered. *Sleeping with some old landlord to pay her rent so she could continue to try and build a career?*

Jones turned and faced Clint.

"Where did you fellas go? If one of my men hadn't seen you go into that restaurant we'd still be looking."

"We're trying to stay out of your hair, Inspector. We moved to the Decatur House."

"Glorified flophouse." Jones snorted.

"It's not bad."

"All of you there?"

"Yep."

"Alibi each other, I suppose."

"For this?" Clint pointed to the girl. "Why would we need alibis for this?"

"Don't tell me, let me guess," Jones said. "It never once occurred to you, for instance, that maybe your good inspector is killing people? Or one of your helpers?"

"Or me?"

"Or you," Jones said, with a nod.

"To tell you the truth, no, it never did occur to me, Inspector."

But it was occurring to him now.

Jones kept Clint around until the two bodies were cleared away. The inspector did not shoo away the onlookers, so Clint figured the policeman wanted them to get a look at him, in case one of them could identify him.

"Walk downstairs with me," Jones said, after the second body was removed.

"Who was the man?" Clint asked.

"A drummer. His sample case is in the room."

"Could he have been the target?"

"Who knows?" Jones asked. "I figure the killer might have entered his room by accident and had to kill him to keep him quiet."

"And why was he naked?"

"Might have had a girl up there at some point, or maybe he just sleeps that way."

"What about him and the girl . . .?"

"The landlord says it was him," Jones said. "One of the other tenants confirmed that the landlord occasionally went to the girl's room and stayed a while. He's a lowlife who preys on these young girls who think they're gonna become the next Lillie Langtry."

When they got downstairs, the landlord took one look at them and found something else to do.

"Let's go outside," Jones said. "Stinks of death in here."

They went out front and Inspector Jones took a deep breath.

"You don't really suspect me, do you?"

"Let's just say you're not high on my list."

"But you suspect Inspector Frost?"

"The killings only started when he got here," Jones pointed out. "What do you think?"

"I think you're right about that," Clint said, "but he's so damned obsessed with catching the killer I just can't see—"

"You're too close," Jones said, "that's why you can't see it."

Clint had to concede that Jones might have a point.

"I'm going to have men watching the Decatur. Don't tell Frost. If it is him and he slips out of the building, we'll follow him. Maybe we can save the next victim."

Clint felt very disloyal to the Scotland Yard inspector but said to the New York inspector, "All right."

FORTY-ONE

"Why didn't you come and get me?" Frost complained.

"I didn't have a chance," Clint said. "The police hustled me right over there."

"Was it the same?" he asked.

"Yes," Clint said, "it was the same."

"And the man?"

"Also strangled. Jones thinks the killer entered his room by mistake, woke him, and had to kill him."

"That's a break in the pattern also, isn't it?" Delvecchio asked. "Two victims at the same time."

"It certainly is," Frost said.

They were outside on the steps to the Dacatur, as there was nowhere inside the building to congregate.

"I think we have to face a reality here," Frost went on.

"What reality?" Clint asked.

"That the killer might be out of control, at this point. He may start piling up victims now, with no rhyme or reason."

"If that's the case," Delvecchio said, "he's gonna make a mistake and get caught."

"I want to catch him," Frost said.

"So do I," Clint said. "I want to put a bullet in his gut and watch him die slowly."

147

He was watching Frost very closely to see how he reacted to this. If the inspector *was* the killer, he was very good, for he betrayed nothing with his face.

Clint again felt disloyal even thinking it, but Inspector Jones was dead right about one thing. The killings had not started until the arrival of Inspector Frost. If the killer had arrived first, by days or perhaps by weeks, why had he not killed during that time?

"So what do we do now?" Eickhorst asked.

"Ask questions, I guess," Clint said.

"And get in the way of the police?" Delvecchio asked.

"Do it discreetly."

"Do the police know where we are staying?" Frost questioned.

"Yes," Clint said, "I had to tell them."

Frost looked around, up and down the street.

"That means they'll be watching us," he said.

"Kind of hard to be discreet while you're being watched," Eickhorst said.

"We'll just have to do the best we can," Clint said.

FORTY-TWO

They decided to split up, making it more difficult for the police to follow them. It was Clint's idea, for two reasons. One, he knew the police would follow Frost, and two, he wanted to be away from Frost for a while so he could make some inquiries.

His guest brought him back down the docks. When he and Frost were both there, the Inspector had made them skip one ship, the one he had come in on. Now Clint wanted to go aboard and see what he could find out.

He once again used the harbormaster to get him in to see the captain, a Swedish man named Pietr Blom.

"Sure, I remember him," said Blom, in only slightly accented English. "Thought he was better than everyone else, he did. Kept to himself. He never told us he was a policeman, though."

Kept to himself. That was what Frost had said the killer would do.

"Do you mind if I talk to some of your crew?"

As with the other ships, the captain said, "If you can find any of them onboard, be my guest."

"Thanks."

• • •

Clint spent half the day questioning crew members, most of whom remembered the "fop" who booked passage to the United States and kept to himself.

"He almost killed Ferdie," one man said, which stopped Clint cold.

"When? How?"

" 'Bout the fourth night out, I think," the man said, scratching his face through hard black-and-gray stubble. "Ferdie decided to try and make friends with the fella. So he started talking to him, followin' him around. Finally, I guess the guy just had enough. He turned on Ferdie and grabbed him by the throat. It took four of us to pull him off. Next day Ferdie had bruises all over his neck, and nobody ever approached the fella again."

"And where's Ferdie now?"

"He took off when we docked," the man said. "For all I know he's been in the same whorehouse for days."

Clint would have liked to talk to Ferdie, but he couldn't very well ask this guy to send Ferdie over to the Decatur. When Frost spotted him he'd know right away that Clint was investigating him.

"Okay," Clint said, "thanks."

He had found out nothing conclusive, but Frost now fit two points of the killer's profile—a profile he, himself, had put forth. First, he had kept to himself on the boat, and second, he was strong enough to strangle a man.

For the first time Clint was seriously starting to consider him a candidate. All those times he looked so tired—was it because he'd been living two lives? Not getting rest at night because he was out prowling the streets for his next victim?

Clint was going to have to bring Delvecchio and Eickhorst in on this. The three of them were going to have to keep watch on the Englishman. If he was the killer, they needed to catch him in the act.

Preferably *before* he killed again.

On his way back to the hotel, Clint suddenly decided to

go to Mulberry Street and talk to Inspector Jones. When he presented himself at the front desk, he was immediately ushered into Jones's office.

"What can I do for you, Mr. Adams?" Jones asked, sitting back in his chair.

"I've been thinking about what we discussed."

"And what was that, exactly?"

"The possibility that Frost could be the killer."

"If he is," Jones said, "he has the perfect cover: the policeman who is out to get the killer. Who'd suspect him?"

"Well, you," Clint said, "and me."

Jones sat straighter.

"It's my job to suspect him," the policeman said. "Tell me why you do."

So Clint told the inspector about his visit to the docks, to the ship that Frost had come in on. When he finished the man was frowning.

"What's wrong?"

"I'm annoyed with myself to have missed that," Jones said frankly. "We didn't know what ship he came in on, and we didn't ask."

"You can't ask everything."

"I'm supposed to," Jones said. "That's my job. Tell me, do we know where this Ferdie is?"

"No," Clint said. "His mates said he was probably holed up at some whorehouse."

"We can check whorehouses," Jones said. "I'll find him and bring him in here. He might be able to tell us something useful."

"Meanwhile, you're having us watched, right?"

"That's right."

"We split up, went four ways. Who would your man follow?"

"Frost."

"All right," Clint said. "I'm going to try something. It

might work and it might not, but if it does—and if Frost *is* the killer—it might put an end to this whole thing.''

"What are you gonna try?"

"I haven't quite figured *that* out, yet.''

FORTY-THREE

When Clint left the police station on Mulberry Street, he went to the nearest saloon. Over a beer, he fretted about suspecting Inspector Frost and possibly being wrong. On the one hand he hoped he was wrong, because he'd hate for Frost to turn out to be the smart killer who'd had him completely fooled. On the other hand, if the killer was Frost, he was going to be carefully watched now, and would probably get caught in a mistake.

The first part was silly. This had nothing to do with his ego, it only had to do with a killer who had claimed four victims since coming to New York. If he was going to get six, was he including the man he might have accidently had to kill last night?

But wait. Everything he'd been told about the killer's pattern had come from Frost. Didn't it stand to reason that if Frost was the killer he'd be steering Clint wrong right from the beginning? Or was he arrogant enough to play fair, figuring no one would ever catch him?

That had to be it. This killer thought he was the smartest man alive. Clint often got that feeling from Frost. Maybe that was the common denominator between the killer and the policeman.

He finished his beer, left the saloon, and went back to

the hotel. He hoped to find Delvecchio and Eickhorst there, but not Frost.

He got his wish.

"We need to talk before Frost comes back," Clint told them. They were in his room, where he had quickly hustled them.

"Why? What's wrong?" Delvecchio asked.

"Just listen to what I'm going to tell you, and wait until I finish before you comment."

They both agreed. Clint told his story—about Jones suspecting Frost and making a good case, about his talk with the crew of the ship, and about what happened when Ferdie tried to make friends.

"So there it is," Clint said. "I may have been helping the killer all along."

"Don't be hard on yourself," Delvecchio said.

"I thought there was something odd about him," Eickhorst, "but I never thought he was the killer."

"And what do you think now?" Clint asked.

"It's a possibility," Eickhorst admitted, then looked at Delvecchio.

"He's cold enough for it," Delvecchio said, "and he's smart—very smart, if he's been steering us in the wrong direction."

"I thought about that, too," Clint said, and spoke of the ego involved.

"You're making a good case to suspect him," Delvecchio said.

"But not for actually believing that it's him," Eickhorst said.

"No," Clint said. "If it's him we're going to have to prove it."

"And how do we do that?" Delvecchio asked.

"We catch him in the act."

"And when do you think that will be?" Eickhorst wanted to know.

"Well, according to *him* it might be tonight."

"But what if he suggested that because he knows he's *not* gonna kill anybody tonight?" Delvecchio pointed out.

"That kind of thinking is going to make me dizzy," Clint said. "Let's just see if we can figure out what he'll do tonight. When he comes back, we can take turns watching him."

"I have a question," Delvecchio said.

"Go ahead."

"What if he doesn't come back?" he asked. "What if he's already out there, stalking his next victim?"

Clint didn't answer right away, then said, "We'll just have to wait and see, I guess."

FORTY-FOUR

Frost turned the corner, saw his three "partners" congregated out front, and went back the way he'd come. He wondered what Clint might have found out down at the docks. There wasn't anything he *could* find out, really. He'd been very careful, except for that one annoying sailor on the ship. If they found him, there might be trouble.

Frost remembered one thing from the ship, and that was the name of the whorehouse most of the men talked about, including Ferdie whatever-his-name-was.

He turned off of Forty-third Street and started down Ninth Avenue. If they were waiting for him they'd have to wait a lot longer. He'd just tell them he thought he had a lead that ultimately didn't pan out.

It was time to visit with Ferdie.

Ferdie Flynn looked down at the top of the brunette's head as she slid his penis in and out of her hot, wet mouth. This was the part of sex he liked the best, *being* satisfied by a woman. When you were on top of them, and inside them, they wanted you to move this way or that way, faster, slower, all these orders that got whispered and then screamed in your ear. This way, however, he got all the pleasure and they couldn't talk because their mouths were full—of him.

And Ferdie knew he was a mouthful. The whores always liked it when he dropped his pants. He had a huge penis and was very proud of it.

"Come on, baby," he said, "make it wet."

Immediately the girl began to slurp, thoroughly wetting his long penis with her saliva.

"Oh, that's it," he said, "I love that sound. Go ahead, baby, enjoy yourself."

If Ferdie thought that Milly Gentry was enjoying herself sucking on his smelly, knobby, vein-ridden cock, he was sorely mistaken. *Jesus,* she'd thought when they first entered the room, *didn't he ever bathe?* Still, he was paying money for a good time and Milly had been a whore a long time. She knew what to do, and as soon as she heard him say how much he liked having his cock sucked that was where she went. Maybe this way she wouldn't end up with him on top of her.

The madam, who went by the name "Flower," if you could believe that, couldn't get a girl who was willing to go with Ferdie, until Milly volunteered. However, she wanted to be paid double, and Flower—the biggest, fattest "flower" Milly had ever seen—agreed.

"It's either that," she said, resignedly, "or come out of retirement and do the guy myself."

Well, now that Milly's mouth was stuffed with Ferdie's cock she was sort of wishing Flower *had* come out of retirement. Usually, when guys came into port and visited the house, they'd been without women for so long that they popped their corks real quick. This one, however, seemed as if he was going to take forever.

Milly reached beneath his testicles, hefting the heavy sack, fondling him, then reached further with the middle finger of her other hand until she was stroking him just short of his asshole. She began bobbing her head up and down, taking him in long, slow strokes and before long he moaned out loud and ejaculated. . . .

•   •   •

Frost waited outside the whorehouse, in an alley across the street. The neighborhood was not that busy and there was not much foot traffic to speak of. He'd stopped one girl who had come out, seemingly finished for the day, and asked about Ferdie, describing him.

"Oh, God, him?" she asked, revulsion plain on her pretty face, "He's upstairs with Milly. She's the only one who'd go with him, but she's old—almost thirty—and trying to make some money to get out of the business."

He thanked the girl and let her go. He'd thought about killing her, but she'd probably forget she ever saw him; besides, she was not a likely victim. He forgot all about her moments later.

Frost knew he was a handsome man, but had no way of knowing the impression he could make on a young woman, even a whore.

He just had enough time to get back to his alley when the door opened and Ferdie appeared. He was hitching up his pants and had a real satisfied look on his face. Frost had heard him tell stories to his mates about how great he was in bed and how women loved him. Frost had taken all of this for a lie, and as Ferdie strutted down the steps he knew—just by looking at him—that he thought he was God's gift to women.

"You are going meet God soon, Ferdie," Frost said beneath his breath, "and he will certainly tell you different."

FORTY-FIVE

"Where is he?" Delvecchio wondered, looking up and down the block.

"He found one," Eickhorst said. "I'm telling you he found one."

Clint hoped not. He was still hoping that Frost wasn't the killer, but had decided the best course of action was to assume that he was.

"We could go look for him," Delvecchio suggested.

"Where?" Clint asked. "Where would you look?"

"Broadway?"

"We tried that. It's hopeless."

They were trying to decide what to do after hours of sitting on the steps and had finally decided to go to dinner when a police coach pulled up in front of the building. They stared at it until Inspector Jones stuck his head out the window.

"Mr. Adams?" he asked. "Would you like to come with me?"

"Where? What for?"

"We might have another victim," Jones said. "I'd like your input."

Clint turned and looked at Delvecchio and Eickhorst. Delvecchio, of the two, was a trained detective.

"I'd like him to come, too," he said, pointing to the man.

"Very well. Bring him."

"Anson, you wait here for Frost."

"What do I tell him?"

"Tell him we're following a lead."

"All right," Eickhorst said, "but hurry back."

Clint and Delvecchio got into the coach with Jones and off they went.

By the time they reached the alley off of Twelfth Street and Eleventh Avenue, Clint and Delvecchio knew what Inspector Jones knew, that a man was dead, apparently strangled.

"Him being strangled was enough for the first policeman on the scene to call for me."

They got out of the coach and walked to the alley, which, by this time, was crowded with police, and onlookers plugging up the entrance.

"Get these people back," Jones said to an officer, who immediately recognized him and said, "Yes, sir."

He, Clint, and Delvecchio entered the alley. The man was fully dressed, lying on his back, with his head at an odd angle.

Jones leaned over him, then stood up.

"Bruising on the neck," he said.

Clint nodded.

"Too much of a coincidence for this not to be the killer's work," he said, "but why? Who was this man?"

"Anybody find a wallet?" Jones asked.

"I did, sir." It was the first officer on the scene, Officer Bolton. He was young, looking barely old enough to shave.

Before anything else could happen, Delvecchio said in Clint's ear, "I've got an idea. I'll be back."

"What else did you find?" Jones asked.

"A letter," the officer said.

"Give them both to me."

Jones accepted the letter and wallet, going through the

latter first, and then handing it to Clint. Neither of them found anything.

"Can't be a robbery with the wallet still here," Jones said. "There's thirty-five dollars in it, and nothing else."

Clint was dimly aware of Jones reading aloud who the letter was addressed to—somewhere in Pennsylvania—and then heard something that made his head snap up when the Inspector read the return address.

"What was that?" he asked.

"Anita—"

"No," Clint said, "the name on the return address."

"Ferdinand Flynn," Jones read.

"Ferdinand?" Clint asked. "Ferdie?"

Jones took the letter out, but didn't read it. Instead he went to the bottom, where the author would have signed his name.

"That's what he signed it, 'Love, Ferdie.' " He looked at Clint. "Do you know this man?"

"I know of him," Clint said. "In fact, I told you about him and you said you'd search the whorehouses for him."

"The sailor who was almost killed on the ship?"

"That's right."

"Well . . ." Jones looked down at the body. "Why kill him now?"

"Because he could identify him."

"To who?"

"To me," Clint said. "After all, I was on that ship asking questions. Inspector, I think I might have gotten this man killed."

"Nonsense," Jones said. "You can't take responsibility for what this sick killer does."

"He obviously thought we might find out something if we talked to this man, and he just as obviously knew where to find him."

"Sailors on long trips often swap stories about their favorite whorehouses," Jones said.

"Then this was my fault, because I didn't ask that question when I was talking to the crew."

"Feel guilty later," Jones said, without sympathy. "Frost obviously heard Ferdie talking about a whorehouse. There must be one around here somewhere. We'll have to go house to house."

"Maybe not, Inspector," Delvecchio said, reappearing.

"What are you talking about?"

"I know this area," Delvecchio said. "There's a whorehouse across the street called The Flower Garden. It's run by a woman called Flower."

Jones looked around at his officers.

"How come nobody knew about this place?"

No one answered.

"Give them a break, Inspector," Delvecchio said. "Maybe they all go home to their wives for it."

Jones thought briefly about going home to his wife for it, but he knew it wouldn't be there.

"Take me to that whorehouse," he ordered.

"It's this way," Delvecchio said. "I just walked over to make sure it was still there, and still in business."

"And is it?"

"As busy as ever."

"Well, let's hope somebody remembers something. . . ." Jones said.

FORTY-SIX

Clint and Jones were both surprised when Delvecchio introduced a big, fat woman as "Flower." She probably weighed three hundred pounds—more if you included the jewelry and the pounds of makeup that was on her face.

"This is your establishment?" Jones asked.

"And who are you?"

He showed her his badge and said, "Police. My name is Inspector Jones."

"Somebody complained about us?" she asked. "I run a clean business, Inspector. No larceny, no—"

"No, no . . . uh, Flower, no one complained. I wanted to ask about a man who might have been here earlier. He's a sailor, and from the looks of him he might even still smell of the sea—"

"Oh, him!" she said, rolling her eyes. "He smelled of more than the sea, let me tell you. I couldn't even get a girl to go upstairs with him until Milly volunteered."

"Milly? Can I see her?"

"Wait right here."

She went through a curtained doorway, into the sitting room, where the whores were on display for the customers. She returned with an attractive, full-bodied brunette who looked thirty-five but was probably closer to thirty.

"Which one is interested?" she asked. "I can't take all three—"

"We're not interested in sex, Milly," Jones said. "The man who you were, uh, with earlier, the sailor?"

"Him?" she said, making a face. "God, did he smell. I don't think he's bathed in a month."

"Then why did you go upstairs with him?" Clint asked.

"I need the money, and Flower said she'd pay me double."

"Did you talk to the man?" Jones asked.

"Only to find out what he wanted."

"Did he tell you anything else?"

"No, nothing. He paid me and didn't even say good-bye. He just left."

Jones turned to Flower.

"Did any of the other girls see him leave?"

"You can ask them."

"Did any of them see anyone else?"

"I don't know, Inspector," Flower said. "Would you like to ask them?"

"Yes, I would."

"Very well," she said, "follow me."

She walked to the curtained doorway again, this time beckoning them through.

Stretched out before them was as impressive an array of female flesh as Clint had seen in a long time.

"Very pretty," Jones said.

"We have only the best here, Inspector."

She was right. The woman they'd talked to, Milly, was probably the only girl in the room over thirty, and as attractive as she was, she was not in the same class as the other girls.

There were five of them. One was a busty blonde who was busting out of her corset; a redhead with fetching freckles across the bridge of her nose and, Clint was willing to bet, on her back; an Oriental girl with long, shiny black hair, like a silk curtain; a black girl who was seemingly all breasts and butt, with caramel-colored skin; and a small girl with her brown hair in pigtails who looked sixteen, but who Clint was willing to bet was twenty-six. If Clint had to pick a girl to spend the afternoon with it would have been the black girl. She was the best-looking one there.

"Girls, these men are policemen," Flower said. "They want to ask you some questions."

"Actually," Jones said, "I'm a policeman. These gentlemen are just colleagues."

"Maybe your colleagues would like to come upstairs while you ask questions?" the blonde asked, eyeing both Clint and Delvecchio.

"Maybe another time, ma'am," Jones said.

"How about you, then?"

"Me? I'm sorry, but I'm married."

"So are half our customers."

"Crystal, you hush up and let the man talk," Flower said.

Crystal fell silent with an amused look on her face.

"Ask your questions, Inspector," Flower said.

"There was a man here with Milly a little while ago," Jones said.

"The smelly one?" the Oriental girl asked.

"That's him."

All the girls wrinkled their noses at the memory.

"Milly, I don't know how you did it," the redhead said. "I woulda gagged, I know it."

"I did it for the money," Milly said, "and I almost did gag."

"This is all very interesting," Jones said, "but I need to know if any of you saw anyone else around here at the same time."

"I had a man in my room," the pigtailed girl said. "I didn't see anything."

"What did that man look like?"

"Like a bank teller," she said. "I guess he was a bank teller."

"Anyone else?"

"I had a man in my room, too," Crystal said. "Tall, barrel-chested, wanted me to do the oddest things to him. He wanted me to—"

"Ah, that's all right," Jones said. "I don't need to know that. No one else?"

The other three girls shook their heads.

"Did anyone see the sailor leave?"

"This curtain is closed, usually," Flower said.

"I saw him leave," the black girl said.

"How did you come to see that, ma'am, with the curtain closed."

"I stuck my head out to say good-bye to Debbie."

"Debbie who?"

"Oh, that's right," Flower said. "Debbie had to go out and run some errands."

"Who is Debbie?" Jones asked again, more forcefully.

"One of our girls."

"And she went before or after the man?"

The girl thought a moment, then said, "Before, but only just."

Jones looked at Clint and Delvecchio.

"She may have seen something." He turned back to Flower. "We need to talk to her. When will she be back?"

"Well, she's running house errands . . ."

"What are house errands?"

"She's doing something for each person in the house, because we can't leave during working hours," Crystal said. "What's this all about?"

"That man Milly was with was found dead in the alley across the street," Jones said. "His name was Ferdinand Flynn."

"I knew he was Ferdie," Flower said. "He introduced himself that way when he came in. Dead? How?"

"He was murdered—strangled."

"Jesus . . ." Crystal said.

"God . . ." Milly said. "He smelled, but I wouldn't want to see him die because of it."

"He died for another reason," Jones said, "and your friend Debbie might die for the same reason. We need to find her."

Flower didn't hesitate.

"Girls, get dressed. We're closed for the rest of the afternoon."

"No, no," Jones objected as the girls surged past them to the stairs. "I have enough men—"

"You don't know where she's going on her errands," Flower said, "and the girls do. They'll help you find her."

Jones looked at Clint, who said, "Send a whore to find a whore."

FORTY-SEVEN

They went out in pairs. Crystal, the blonde, went with Delvecchio. The redhead, Amy, went with Clint. The Oriental girl, who went by the name Golden Lee—"You can call me Goldie"—went with Inspector Jones, who seemed to be nervous about it. The other girls went together, and Flower stayed behind.

"I don't move around much, anymore," she said, and waved them off.

Delvecchio and Crystal went to the garment district. Crystal said that Debbie had to pick up some costumes for the girls.

"She was already here," the man at the costume place said, "been and gone."

"Where to now?" Delvecchio asked her.

"Well, Amy and your friends are checking the post office. The Inspector and Goldie are checking the market. She had one more stop after that."

"Well, where was it?"

Crystal looked panicky and said, "I can't remember."

Inspector Jones and Goldie got to the post office, on Thirty-third Street and Eighth Avenue, and started looking for

Debbie. The post office was huge, the largest in the country, and it was busy.

"What's she look like?" Jones asked.

"Real pretty, not tall, long brown hair," Goldie said. "She was wearing a blue dress."

"What kind of blue?"

"Um, not too vivid blue," Goldie said. "Maybe sky blue?"

Jones swiveled his head back and forth, searching for her among the crowd. He was startled when Goldie put her hand on his arm. He turned and looked into her almond-shaped eyes, and at that moment he wasn't nervous anymore. In fact, he admitted to himself that he would have liked nothing more than to go back to the house and spend the rest of the day and night in bed with her.

And she knew it.

"Don't worry," she said. "We'll find her."

FORTY-EIGHT

Clint and Amy were in the middle of the market. Clint could smell the commingled odors of fresh vegetables and fresh fish.

"Was this the last place she was coming to?" he asked Amy.

"I would think so," she said. "After all, she's buying food. She'd have to get it home quickly."

"And she was alone? Doing all this shopping?"

"She would have grabbed a cab and had the driver help her," Amy said. "Debbie can get men to do anything she wants."

"I'll bet the same is true of y—of all of you."

"Why, thank you, Mr. Adams," she said. "What a nice compliment."

"Don't kid me, Amy," he said. "You all know you're gorgeous."

"Maybe we do," she said, "but it's nice to hear it from a man once in a while."

"I guess you're right."

They were both scanning the crowd while they were talking.

"We don't get many men who give compliments," she said. "They just want what they want and that's it."

Clint found himself looking at Amy's profile. She had high cheekbones; big, beautiful green eyes; a slender, pretty nose; and a wide, full-lipped mouth. She was about five foot eight, slender but with full breasts. She turned her head and caught him looking at her, and smiled.

"What?"

"I was just thinking of another compliment, but I didn't want to push it."

"Go ahead," she said, facing him straight on, "push it."

"Well, I think you're very—"

"Blue!" she said.

"That's not what—"

"Blue, I see blue," she repeated, looking over his shoulder.

"Where?" he asked.

She grabbed his hand and said, "Come on."

She ran, pulling him along, swerving to avoid other people as she tried to keep her eyes on the patch of sky blue she had seen.

"It's her," she said, as she suddenly got a clear look. "Debbie! Debbie!"

It took a little more yelling, but Debbie finally turned around and waved at Amy with a big smile.

Thank God, Clint thought, they'd found her before Frost did.

"Handsome," Debbie said to Jones, Clint, and Delvecchio, "and blond—and he talked with a funny accent."

"British?" Jones asked.

"I've never heard a British accent before," she said, tilting her head to one side. "Can someone do one for me?"

They were back at the whorehouse, questioning Debbie about the man who had asked her questions about the dead man.

"I don't have to see the dead man, do I?" she'd asked, when they requested her help.

"No," Jones said, "just answer a few questions, miss."

"All right," she'd said.

"I don't know if any of us can do—" Jones started, but he stopped when Delvecchio spoke up.

"It's something like this," he said, took a moment to think, and then repeated, "It's something like this," with a British accent.

"Do that again," Clint said.

"It's something—"

"No, say something else." He looked at Debbie. "What did he ask you?"

"If I knew whether there was a sailor inside with one of the girls."

Clint looked at Delvecchio, who repeated the line with an uncanny British accent.

"Where did you learn to do that?"

Delvecchio shrugged.

"I've been listening to Frost," he said. "I can do pretty good Mexican, and Italian, and a few others."

"Could we finish up here?" Jones asked.

"Sorry," Clint said. He looked at Debbie. "Was that it?"

"That was it exactly," she said.

"And what did you tell him?"

"That I knew Milly was with this sailor who smelled. He looked real happy when I told him that."

"And then you left?"

"Yep, just walked away."

They were in the sitting room, and the rest of the girls were up in their rooms.

"Can I go now?"

"Sure," Jones said, "you can go. I might need you to identify the man, though."

"The live one?" she asked, hopefully.

"Yes," he said, "the live one."

After she left the room, Jones asked Delvecchio and Clint, "Are you thinking what I'm thinking?"

"I'm thinking why didn't he kill her, too?" Clint said.

"I'm thinkin' about the girls upstairs in their bedrooms,"
Delvecchio said. Both men stared at him. "Hey, I'm in the
mood. Sue me. It's this place."

"Speaking of which," Jones said, "let's get out of here
before I do something I'll regret."

FORTY-NINE

Frost knew he'd made a mistake, and it was a stupid one. He'd left the girl alive.

Eickhorst was very evasive about where Clint and Delvecchio had gone. So evasive, in fact, that he knew something was wrong. Then he realized that they'd probably gone looking—for what? Clint had gone to the docks . . . of course! He'd gone to check the ship Frost had come in on. In doing that, he'd probable gotten Ferdie Flynn's name. And where would they have told him to look for Ferdie? A whorehouse. The only question was, did they know which whorehouse? If they did, and they went there, they'd not only find Ferdie across the street, but they'd find the girl he had talked to.

Stupid, he told himself, stupid, stupid, stupid. It was an oversight to leave the girl alive, and a costly one, at that.

He stood up and walked to the door of his room. Eickhorst had gone to his room at the same time Frost had gone to his. He opened the door and headed down the hall to the other man's room.

Clint, Delvecchio, and Inspector Jones ran into the Decatur and up the stairs. They stopped in front of Eickhorst's room just long enough to knock. When there was no answer they tried the door. Finding it locked the three of them forced it open.

"Jesus," Delvecchio said. "That son of a bitch!"

Eickhorst was on the floor at the foot of the bed. He was wearing his shirt and jeans, but no boots. The bed was made, but messed up some. He'd probably been resting, or even taking a nap. There was a gun on the end table next to the bed. His neck was bruised. He'd been strangled, but his neck wasn't broken.

Jones leaned down over the fallen comrade and said, "He's dead."

"No!" Delvecchio said. "I'll kill that son of a bitch!"

Jones stood up and said, "You're going to have to find him, first."

Clint and Delvecchio watched the police carry Eickhorst's body from the Decatur. Jones was standing by, as well.

"It's Frost," he said. "It's got to be. I'll have this city covered to find him. I *hate* dirty policemen, even if they are from another country."

"I agree," Clint said. "Frost."

"I'll kill him," Delvecchio muttered.

"Mr. Delvecchio," Jones said. "Now that we pretty much know who the killer is, I'd appreciate it if you went back to Brooklyn."

"Are you tellin' me to get out of town?"

"No," Jones said, "just Manhattan, until I catch this guy."

"If you think—"

"If you don't go, I'll have you locked up. Is that clear?"

Delvecchio paused, then nodded. "Clear." He looked at Clint. "Don't leave New York without saying good-bye."

"I won't," Clint promised.

Delvecchio turned and left the building. Clint did not believe, for one minute, that the man was going back to Brooklyn.

He wondered if Jones did.

FIFTY

Clint stayed in the Decatur that night, even though there were ghosts there now. The ghost of Anson Eickhorst, the ghost of the Scotland Yard inspector that David Frost had once been. It occurred to him before going to bed that, with the two victims today, that made six. The killer—Frost—had gotten his six. Would he be satisfied? Would he now leave New York to go to a new place and start over?

If he did, he'd find police waiting for him. They were watching every avenue out of town. There was no way he could get on a train without them seeing him.

He looked down at the long, lean—but big-breasted—redhead in bed next to him. Amy had been very understanding when he'd told her he didn't really feel like sleeping alone that night. He also told her that he never paid for sex before, and wasn't going to start now.

"That's fair," she said. "I owe you one, anyway."

"Owe me one for what?" he asked.

"The compliment."

He laughed.

"All it takes is a compliment?"

"From you, yes . . ."

And so she was there, next to him. They'd had sex twice, very energetic sex, during which he found she was totally

uninhibited. Also, he'd been right about her freckles. They
were on the slopes of her breasts, and sprinkled across her
back. He looked down at that back now, as she slept on
her stomach. He put his hand on her ass, feeling the
smooth, hot skin beneath his palm, but he didn't wake her.

He got out of bed and walked to the window. He still
couldn't sleep. Frost was out there, somewhere.

He moved the curtain aside and looked down at the
street. He thought he saw something, waited, and saw it
again. In a darkened doorway across the street someone was
smoking a cigarette. He could see the glow when they inhaled.

Son of a bitch.

He dressed and went downstairs. He made his way to the
back of the building and found the rear door. He let himself
out, then crept around the side of the building as quietly as
he could. Would Frost be arrogant enough to come here?
Oh, yes, he would. He had to pay Clint back, because it
was Clint he would blame for his downfall.

And of all the places the police were *not* watching, this
was it.

There was an alley next to the Decatur. Clint took it to
the street, paused to pinpoint the location of the cigarette.
Frost was inviting him in.

He moved in the darkness down the street and then
crossed over. Quietly, he made his way back until he was
just feet away from the doorway. At that moment the man
in the doorway inhaled, and in the glow of the cigarette
Clint could see it wasn't Frost. It was a drunk, propped up
against the door, smoking a cigarette—and it looked like
he was doing it in his sleep.

"Shit," he said aloud.

"My sentiments exactly, old boy," Frost said from behind him. "You didn't think I'd leave without saying good-
bye, did you, Clint? After the team we made?"

Clint felt the barrel of a gun pressed hard against his

spine. Frost took Clint's gun from his hand and dropped it to the ground.

"That's the Navy Colt you feel, old boy, not that little gun you gave me."

"Frost—"

"What?" Frost asked, cutting him off. "What could you possibly want to say to me, Clint?"

"You're sick," Clint said. "Let us help you."

"Help me?" Frost said. "You want to kill me, Clint. You've said it over and over again. And I'll bet Delvecchio wants to, also, since I killed his dear friend Mr. Eickhorst."

"Why'd you do that, Frost?" Clint asked. "Why'd you have to kill him? You had your six."

"You think the number matters?" Frost asked. "I'll tell you the absolute truth, Clint. I don't know why I kill people, I really don't. But I know why I killed Mr. Eickhorst."

"Oh? Why?"

"To get back at you," Frost said, pressing the barrel harder again his back. "You went to the docks, didn't you? Talked to the crew of the ship I came in on? They told you about me?"

"Only that you'd almost killed Ferdie. You should have killed him onboard and dumped him over. Killing him here was stupid. Leaving the girl alive was even more stupid. And by killing Eickhorst, you've assured your own death."

"Threats?" Frost asked. "Who are you to be making threats?"

"There's a gun on you right now, Frost. Can't you feel it?"

Frost's eyes flicked left, right, and up.

"You're bluffing."

"Delvecchio's out there with a gun. You don't think I'd come out here alone, do you?"

"Yes, I do," Frost said. "You're the arrogant cowboy."

"And you're the arrogant Brit," Clint said, "but you've started to make mistakes, Inspector Frost, and tonight you made the biggest one of all."

"Turn around, you bloody gobshite! I want you to see this coming."

Clint turned and could barely see Frost's face in the faint moonlight.

"You have to cock the hammer, Inspector Frost. If you do, Delvecchio will fire. You'll never get to pull the trigger."

Clint could see the flicker of doubt in the man's eyes.

"Give me the gun, David," Clint said. "You're a sick man. I'll get you help. I won't kill you. I won't let Delvecchio kill you. I'll get you the help you need."

For a moment he thought he had him, but then he saw the jaw set firmly.

"I don't need your bloody help," Frost said, and cocked the hammer back on the Navy Colt.

The shot came instantly. When the bullet smacked into Frost's side his eyes bugged out. He might have been able to pull the trigger of his own gun, but Clint moved quickly, disarming him and breaking his arm in the process.

Of course that didn't matter, because by the time he hit the ground he was dead.

Delvecchio came out of the shadows, still holding his gun.

"How'd you know I was out there?" he asked Clint.

"I didn't, really," Clint said. "I just didn't think you'd go back to Brooklyn so peacefully."

"Well," Delvecchio said, looking down at the dead Englishman, "you were right about that."

Watch for

THE BORTON FAMILY GANG

214th novel in the exciting GUNSMITH series
from Jove

Coming soon!

J. R. ROBERTS
THE GUNSMITH